Everythin

Socrates Adams was born in Bath in 1984. He currently lives in Manchester. *Everything's Fine* is his first novel.

'Hilarious and unsettling and one thousand per cent original. I have never read anyone who is anything like Adams. I laughed more than I can remember laughing. A sad weight settled in my chest. As fresh as veganism. That space on Mount Rushmore is waiting for Adams' face.'

Ben Brooks, author of *Grow Up*.

'What if I were to tell you that you could read a book that absolutely nails 21st-century office-dick alienation, that'll make you laugh out loud and cry inside all at the same time, and that's written by an author with the coolest name in the whole GD world? Is that something you might be interested in?'

Gavin James Bower, author of *Dazed & Aroused.*

'Socrates Adams speaks for a generation. *Everything's Fine* explores the horror and the humour of the everyday with humane observation and fearless wit.'

Jenn Ashworth, Author of *A Kind of Intimacy* and *Cold Light.*

Everything's Fine

Socrates Adams

Transmission Print
www.transmissionprint.com

First published in 2012 by
Transmission Print
Rhos on Sea, Conwy

Printed and bound in by
CPI Group (UK) Ltd, Croydon CR0 4YY

*All characters in this publication are fictitious and any
resemblance to real persons, living or dead, is purely
coincidental.*

A CIP catalogue record for this book is available from the
British Library.

ISBN 978-0-956658319

For Emma and Brian

I have a physical presence.
I have mental ability.
I am a human being.
I am permanent.

PART 1

Shirt tie shoes jacket. Here I am. Sitting nervously in a room on the top floor of the office. This is my boss's floor. I am waiting for my superior to come and assess my performance over this last month. My performance has not been good. My performance has been bad.

The assessment room is made of marble and gold. There is a platinum fountain full of champagne. There are gargoyles pointing out from the top corners of the room. The table is covered with fur and has elephant tusks for legs.

Everything in here is prohibitively expensive. That means you are prohibited from touching it.

My boss enters the room. My boss is a little stocky moustachioed man. He is a little stocky athlete and would look great hurling bowling balls around. He would love to throw the bowling balls

1

at human beings. He would love to play rugby with the heads of human beings. He would kick the human heads so far over the goal posts they would never be seen again. He is wearing a little ribbon on his chest that means he is committed to stopping cancer in its tracks.

If he threw the heavy bowling ball at your head you would think before it hit you: great technique.

He sits down.

'Ian, we are here to talk about your performance this last month. Your performance this last month has been terrible. Do you have your Targets and Actuals?'

I bring out a sheet of paper with two sets of numbers on it. One set of numbers is my Targets. This is a set of very high numbers and percentages. The other set of numbers is my Actuals. This is a set of very low numbers and percentages.

My boss looks at the sets of numbers. He looks at me. His eyes are very big and white. He carefully removes a bottle of red ink and an old fashioned pen from the drawer in front of him.

I think he has lovely and delicate fingers. His fingers look like dancers.

'Ian. I am going to mark the areas you've under-performed in with this red ink.'

He places the sheet down flat on the desk. He threads his fingers together before cracking his knuckles, then picks up the ink and holds it above the sheet.

He pours the entire pot of red ink over the paper. Red ink pours over the desk and over my shoes and the floor. I look at the red ink soaking into the fur and staining the marble floor. I look at the gold and the gargoyles and the platinum. Anywhere except my boss's face.

I pick up the dripping red sheet and try to take this extensive feedback on board. I make an expression with my hands and face which tells my boss, 'I am thinking about this and taking it all on board'. I hope my boss can hear the sincere and heartfelt thoughts about changing my life.

I am having the most intense and sincere feelings that any worker has ever had. I am 110% sincere.

'How do you feel about this feedback, Ian? Do you think that it's fair feedback?'

'I sincerely think I definitely need to make a change in my life.' I say, carefully.

'I think it might be too late for that, Ian.' He leans forward on the desk. 'Why do you do this job?'

'For the excellent pay and fantastic career opportunities.'

'The money and prospects are only good if you hit your targets, Ian. Have you worked out how much money your basic salary gives you for each hour you work?'

'No.'

'I have. You earn £5.60 per hour. You never hit your targets. I always hit my targets. I earn

£5.60 per second.'

Targets are a very important part of the job I do and are a very important part of everything outside of work as well. You should hit every target you set yourself. I sell tubes to people who need tubes for carrying fluids from one location to another, using either gravity or a pump. It is important to know whether a pump is going to be used or not. If a pump is going to be used then the tube has to be slightly thicker to cope with the additional pressure. Thicker plastic means mega-bucks-target-smashing-success-power-winner. I am programmed for success.

Sometimes I lie to people and tell them they need the thicker tubes even when they don't. This is called having a *sales story* or being *creative*. These are technical sales terms so I understand if you don't understand them.

Once, one of my clients found out about my sales story and made a complaint. The company supported me completely and told him I was new and stupid and incompetent and had no idea about tubes and that they were going to fire me.

'The reason you are doing so badly, I think, is your lack of discipline. When I was working at your level I was the most disciplined worker of all time, but I'm no hero and I'd be the first to admit that.'

He is always so hard on himself.

'One thing I am,' he continues, 'is seriously disciplined. I am a disciple of discipline. You lack

4

discipline and have no responsibilities. I have made a bespoke package to teach you discipline.'

He takes out a small grey tube. It is eight inches long and two point five inches across. It is a standard tube. It is worth twelve point eight pence if you buy less than a hundred. It is worth ten point two pence if you buy more than a hundred. It is a heavy duty tube.

'This is a tube. You have to imagine this tube is your baby.'

'My baby?'

'Yes, your baby. What would you like to call your beautiful bouncing baby?'

'Can I just call it Tube?'

'No. You have to call it a real name. A name like Mildred. Call it Mildred.'

'Okay. Hello, Mildred.'

I put my hand on top of Mildred. It feels awkward. I take my hand off her and immediately I want to put it back.

'You have to carry Mildred with you at all times, to understand the burden of having someone totally dependent on you. Whenever you meet people you have to say, "This is my baby, Mildred" so you can understand how embarrassing you are.'

I hold Mildred up in front of my face. I turn her around a few times. I look through her hole. She is one long hole, I suppose.

'How long do I have to look after Mildred?'

'Until you learn about responsibility and

discipline.'

Human emotions are so difficult to understand. I feel oddly proud and utterly worthless.

Will she move to the country? Will she start her own business? Will she own a holiday home in the alpine peaks of France?

All of these questions trouble me as I look down at Mildred, looking up at me. Being a father is so god-damn difficult. That's what I am discovering now that Mildred is in my life.

I leave Mildred on her bed and eat some breakfast before work. I am getting into the habit of eating unsweetened muesli for breakfast because of the slow-release energy it provides throughout the day. It's the complex carbohydrates.

I live in a very small flat. There is almost nothing in the flat. Just me and a television and Mildred.

I am halfway through my daily strengthening exercises when my phone makes a noise. I check it. A little envelope is flashing on the screen. Looks like an angry envelope.

DO NOT LEAVE MILDRED ALONE
WHILE YOU EAT YOUR BREAKFAST
AND DO EXERCISES AND CHECK

YOUR MESSAGES. SHE MIGHT
SUFFER FROM COT DEATH.

It is from my boss.

I move from the living room into the
bedroom. Mildred is lying on the bed in front of
me and does not look like she is suffering from cot
death.

My bedroom is a tight cream box. There is a
door in it. There is a bed. There is a light. Little
grey Mildred looks lonely and impatient, lying on
the bed. I scoop her up and cradle her out of the
bedroom. I am not sure how I am meant to do
exercises while carrying Mildred. Maybe this is
why a lot of parents are fat.

I sit on the sofa, naked, holding Mildred. I
want to put on clothes but I can't, not without
putting Mildred down. I want to eat my muesli, but
I can't, not without putting Mildred down. I want
to put Mildred down. I receive a text message.

DO NOT PUT MILDRED DOWN.

Successful parents manage to balance the
needs of their children with their own
requirements. I have to come up with an elegant
and simple solution that allows me to carry on as
normal while knowing where Mildred is at all
times.

I shove Mildred under my armpit and look
around. I attach Mildred to my chest with sticky-

tape.

Now I can relax and eat my breakfast while I watch the morning news.

Being interested in current affairs is an important part of being a grown-up. When I was a child I thought current affairs were very boring. That is why it is so important to be interested in them as a grown-up.

It shows everyone how mature I am.

I'm not interested in comics, or cartoons, or music videos. I just like to make myself watch the news.

I look at the time and notice I am running a little late. This is due to the pressures of being a single father. I throw on my suit and step out of the door. It smells of the city out here, the same smell as my house, the same smell as at work. I walk through the sunshine for ten minutes, dodging the early-morning traffic, then I push through the doors to my office floor.

'Hi guys!'

That's what I think to myself as I say nothing to everyone I pass, keeping my eyes to the ground. I am a real character. The people I work with are intrigued by me. They must think, 'there goes the enigma'.

I don't talk to them much because I feel it encourages an apathetic atmosphere in the office. Business needs to be streamlined and dynamic. Business is money and money is business.

My desk. The launch pad for my assault on

high-profile blue-chip companies. This is where the magic happens. If there is anyone out there who needs tubes and doesn't currently have a preferred supplier of tubes, I will do my best to make sure we can, in the future, provide them with all the tubes they could ever need.

My phone beeps as I receive another message.

WHERE IS MILDRED?

I don't know where she is. I think hard. I know where she is.

She is still strapped to my chest. My heart is beating an inch away from Mildred's head.

I need to get her out of there.

The people who work on the same pod as me are looking over and saying hello. I smile at my sales team. I start to sweat. I look at Brian, the most senior person on the desk.

I say, 'Toilet. Ha!'

There are no cubicles available except for the larger cubicle for disabled people. I look around before ducking inside.

I remove my jacket, shirt and tie. I yank the sticky tape away from my chest, leaving Mildred dangling, half stuck to my side. She is covered in sweat.

I should get a papoose.

Will I move to the country? Will I start my own business? Will I own a holiday home in the alpine peaks of France?

I have been badly abused these past three days. I have been burned. I have been left in a cupboard. I have been squashed under an armpit and then suffocated against a disgustingly fat chest.

Ian is looking at me. He brings me level with his face and turns me over. His palms are like beef cooked pink. Warm, sweaty and tender. He feels horrible. I think Ian destroyed himself a long time ago. I imagine it was a pathetic, passive self-destruction. He never did anything wrong. He never did anything right. He never did anything.

I feel his breath on me.

Ian does not stand up for himself. He has no idea about anything or anyone. I watch the other people he works with look at him and laugh and talk about him together. I can't imagine what he must be thinking to himself.

They are looking at him holding me up to his face and breathing on me. He looks nervously around and then puts me down on the desk.

I feel like a toy. I feel like he won't ever use me in the way I am meant to be used. I think maybe I am going to be a toy until the end of time.

I would very much like it if he could put me into the plumbing somewhere. I am a part of the world, Ian, and I want you to put me into the plumbing, please.

I undo the top button of my shirt.

The day is really starting to heat up. Brian has made a sale. When someone makes a sale, everyone in the office cheers and they ring a bell. There is a television in the corner of the room. My boss's face appears on the television, bigger than life size.

The video of my boss's face winks at us all and he says, 'Have a laugh, then get back to work!' We all have a good laugh and then get back to work. I look over at Brian. He is a great guy. He is wearing a simple, pink tie. Brian has a great instinct for fashion.

I look at the other people on my pod. There are four other people. One of them is called Mark. He is new. He gets teased because he is new! It's not bullying because he laughs about it. He is a great guy and a good sport.

The other people on my pod are Eric, Gavin and Jo. The six of us make up a sales team. We go on team nights out and have a great time. We are all great friends.

I look at Brian and say,

'Nice one, Brian. How many did you sell?'

Brian looks at me for a second and then looks away. I wait for him to turn back to speak to me. He starts making another call. While he waits to get through to someone he turns around to Mark and starts talking to him.

'How many did you sell, Brian?' I ask again.

He gets through to the person he is calling. He

probably sold loads. He doesn't look at me.

I wonder about what the guys think of me. They think I am just one of the guys. They think I am an important part of the team.

Mildred is sitting next to my computer, watching me sell. It is strange to have a companion in my life. It has been years since I've had someone to spend my time with. It makes me philosophical, having someone around all of the time.

It makes me think deep thoughts like, 'What's so great about having someone around all the time? Do human beings need someone else around to be themselves? Are personalities relative?'

I am sometimes staggered by how impressively profound I can be.

It is surprising that I haven't had someone to share my life with for such a long time. Rapport is one of the things that is most important when you are trying to attract a romantic partner or a non-romantic friend.

I have been on hundreds of industry-approved courses to help me improve my rapport-building skills. I have scored consistently highly in both the theory and practical elements.

I feel like I should be in a situation where so many people want to experience my rapport-building skills that I have the luxury of subjecting them to advanced filtering and selection systems.

That is not the situation I am in.

I don't know why. I am an active listener. I

know the sales structure. All human interaction is sales. I am going to sell my personality and physical traits to you by the way we interact. I am going to build genuine, warm rapport with you. I am going to ask you hundreds of open questions, so you can't say yes or no, and our conversation will never end. I am going to prove I am an active listener by repeating everything you say to me back to you in a condensed way. We are going to be great friends.

I remember the first sales course I attended. I was apprehensive at the time because I was under the impression that some people might view salesmen as a bit of a nuisance. What shocked me was the confidence of the trainer. He explained that people love to be sold to. They love it.

Ever since then I have been the most confident, delightful, engaging salesman in the history of time.

Brian is talking to Mark about me. They are laughing about me. I put my headset on and get ready to make an excellent call.

It is always great to arrive home after a hard day at the office. Because of the way I am trying to work at the moment, every day is a hard day. I am just testing myself so god-damn hard at the moment.

At work we get incredibly detailed and

comprehensive targets. We are targeted on number of calls made; number of tubes sold; percentage of tubes sold at more than twelve pence per tube; length of tubing sold; number of clients visited; amount of hours spent on the phone; number of coffee breaks taken; number of toilet breaks taken; money earned versus time spent earning money; amount of overtime worked; waist size; I.Q; non-work e-mails sent; work e-mails sent.; letters sent and time spent between calls.

Because of these targets I can live a life that is well-managed, organised and efficient. The targets are all related to each other. It is very difficult to decide which target to concentrate on. If you miss any of these targets there tends to be a knock-on effect which makes you miss all of your targets. For example, if you take too many coffee breaks it means you will take too many toilet breaks, which means you will spend less time on the phone, which means you will sell less tubes, which means you are more desperate to sell tubes, which means that you will sell the tubes too cheaply, which means you'll be stressed and take more coffee breaks!

Basically, everything comes down to coffee breaks.

Does I.Q affect amount of coffee required?

Even I don't quite understand the targets perfectly.

I need a new target: Mildred happiness percentage.

14

I am sitting and thinking about how to measure the Mildred happiness percentage. I am watching a programme about a famous person. I think they are being interviewed by another famous person. Mildred is in the other room, sleeping.

I change the channel. Now I am watching a woman stepping onto a plastic board and stepping off again. I wish I had the plastic board to step on to. I stand up from the chair and look into the mirror. I am overweight. I spend a few minutes sucking in my cheeks to make myself look thinner. I think that even if I sucked my cheeks inside out, I would still look overweight.

Taste is a pleasure that doesn't fade, regardless of how old you become. That's why I love food so much. I imagine myself as an old guy, eating pasta and chips and chocolate. The flavour will be just the same, just as good. I imagine feeling melancholic, looking back, remembering this imagined future.

Being cuddly is just who I am. It's part of my trustable, lovable image.

I think a lot about how the people I know would react if I lost a lot of weight. I think they might say things like,

'Wow. You look great, Ian.'

And then I would say,

'Thanks, Brian.'

I feel my phone vibrate. I struggle to get my hand in my pocket. There is a message waiting.

WHERE IS MILDRED?

The message is from my boss. I walk into the other room to find Mildred. There she is!

But she is not on the bed.

She has rolled onto the floor with the dust and hair.

I pick Mildred up and look at my precious child. I rock her in my arms. Another text message comes through for me.

> YOU NEED TO BUY A COT FOR
> MILDRED. YOU NEED TO BUY A
> PRAM FOR MILDRED. YOU ARE
> MAKING ME ANGRY.

'Don't worry,' I say to Mildred, 'I'm going to buy you a pram and a cot, so you don't fall out of bed again.'

Mildred looks back at me and says nothing. I wonder whether she can understand me. Love is universal, unimpeded by language. Love is attained after a certain period of intimate rapport-building.

> STOP SPEAKING TO THE TUBE.
> IT'S A TUBE, NOT YOUR BABY.
> FEEL ASHAMED OF YOURSELF.

I feel ashamed.

My finger is hovering over the autodial button. I am hovering above the autodial button. I have been hovering above for maybe five minutes. The autodial button is blowing air at me. The air is making me hover. The autodial button looks sexy to my finger. Autodial. Auto-Erotic Dial. It is a pair of lips that I am going to plunge my finger between.

I love the autodial button. It makes me feel dangerous whenever I press it. It feels dangerous. It is the same as playing Russian roulette.

My worst nightmare is an angry Scottish person on the other end. I am not racist. I just cannot understand Scottish people on the phone sometimes.

I hear a strange, buzzing ring. It takes me six seconds to realise it is my phone, ringing. It is very rare for a client to ring back asking about the excellent quality of our tubes.

I pick up the phone. Through the receiver I hear a noise. It is my boss making the noise. My boss is making the noise at me. The noise is a word. That word is my name. My name is Ian.

'Ian.'

'Yes, boss?'

'Come up to the room.'

'Yes, boss.'

I wait by the lift for a long time. The room is on the fifteenth floor of the office. People who walk by me while I wait for the lift seem to know something I don't. Some of them laugh to each other.

Finally, the three red lights on the lift button go out and I can step in and travel up. Mildred is in my pocket.

I am in the room. This is the first time I have been in this room on my own. I feel lonely. There is a red stain on the fur of the table and a faded red mark on the marble of the floor.

My boss arrives. I don't feel lonely any more. I feel dead.

'Sit down.'

'I am sitting down.'

'Oh,' my boss looks at me. He is angry. 'That's weird. People normally stand up when I enter the room.'

I stand up. My boss sits down, makes a note in a black book, then begins to speak. I'm still standing up.

'Do you know why we have autodial buttons, Ian?'

'To save time.' I say, with confidence.

'No. It's so that people like you, with no qualifications, can use the phones, Ian. I want to talk to you about why you were not using your autodial function. Even for someone with no qualifications, Ian, you are very stupid. Why don't you have any qualifications, Ian?'

'I do not perform well under exam conditions.'

'You do not perform well under any conditions.'

My boss looks fantastic.

'You know, Ian, I am really amazed by your lack of progress. You can't even successfully press a button. Pressing a button is one of the easiest things in life. It's a small button, Ian. Why can't you press a small button? What is wrong with you, Ian?'

He looks angry, like an owl. I am a vole. Voles are like mice but smaller, weaker, and more likely to be killed by owls.

I think something bad is going to happen. I think I should have made a will. Mildred won't have any chance of a normal life if something happens to me.

'Ian. I have put a huge amount of money and effort into giving you good opportunities at this company.'

I feel a wave of appreciation and tenderness towards my boss. My heart is fluttering on stringy wings.

'But it hasn't worked out. I am going to have to demote you.'

'I thought I was already at the lowest possible level.'

'That's the problem. I have had to create a new job title.'

I am still standing up.

'What's lower than Extremely Junior Tube Salesman?'

'Ian, from now on your job title is: Tiny Shit Head.'

Tiny Shit Head. I feel something tugging my guts.

'Is there a Job Description?'

I am thinking about the permanence of different types of plastic. I am imagining millions of tonnes of rainwater gushing through tubes. I am thinking about the type of plastic that does not even corrode when splashed with sulphuric acid. It's called Acrylonitrile Butadiene Styrene.

Ian starts talking to me.

'Mildred, you mustn't worry about our financial circumstances.'

I remain motionless on the high chair. He lifts some food up to my mouth and then he shoves it inside me.

I am a turkey, being stuffed ready for basting and roasting. Baste me with sulphuric acid, I think.

After stuffing me, he collects the waste product from my private areas without even averting his eyes.

'You know, it's weird having you around,' he manages somehow to talk and eat without choking. 'I haven't really had anyone to discuss things with for ages. It just gets me thinking about what is important in life. Sure, I've got my sales skills, that's something I will always have, but what else have I achieved? A lot of people take time out after university and go travelling, or do charity work or something like that. Seeing you every day, it makes me think, if I had the time over again, what would I do differently?'

Ian looks like a cow. He is chewing and thinking. He looks like a plump little cow with a mouth full of grass.

'I think I want to see parts of the world I haven't seen before. I want to take you with me to see the world.'

I want to tell Ian that I have already travelled quite a lot. I am from the Yuyao Jiayuan Hydraulics Tube Factory in China. I have been hauled across country from factory to port; I have been shipped across grey, rolling oceans; I have seen whales breach and heard their songs, distant through the hulls of huge tankers; through portholes I have seen remote islands, maelstroms, pirates, idyllic skies. Up and down through wave and sky and spray and mist and cloud and ice and snow and sun.

Ian would not understand.

'I'm thinking: Alps. I'm thinking: France. I'm thinking: French Alps.'

He brings out a photo of a snow-covered mountain. It is not a mountain from the Alps.

'I am trying to decide whether to learn to ski. What do you think?'

I remain motionless and silent. I want to roll off the table and into someone else's kitchen. Why can't he slot me into the plumbing somewhere and get it over with? All I want to do is help to transfer some fluids from somewhere to somewhere else.

'I start my new job tomorrow. I'm not sure what I'm going to be doing.'

You are going to be doing the same thing that you were doing yesterday. Except you are going to be working even harder. You are going to be working for even less money. You are going to be even worse at it.

'I've got some ideas for making some money, Mildred, don't worry. I found some sites on the internet that have some very interesting leads on them.'

He is looking at me with earnest, loving eyes. They always seem red-rimmed and watery. His phone makes a noise and he looks down at it before looking a little bit upset. He glances around as if to check whether anyone is watching us, before scooping me up and taking me into the bedroom.

I lie awake for a while thinking about my old life and my new life. Ian is tossing and turning. I am drifting off as I hear him say, softly,

'Mildred.'

I can't help but think what pathetic creatures human beings are, and what a terrible world they have created for themselves.

login: iantrouble

password: *******

Welcome to the members-only area of the site. Soon you will be eligible to earn real money completing surveys for our clients. Our clients value the opinions of ordinary hard-working human beings like you. The first step is to complete one of the introductory surveys you will find below, so we can build up a picture of which demographic group you belong to. It should take no longer than 5 – 40 minutes depending on the survey, your reading ability and the length of your answers. Please select a survey:

1. Your household
2. Products that you use
3. Important events in your life
4. Sports and leisure
5. Politics and power
6. Your job

Important events in your life
Please answer the following questions as honestly as possible. If you do not answer honestly you will not be eligible for any money.

When did you leave school? - Over five years ago.

Why did you leave school? - To be a salesman and make a lot of money selling tubes.

Do you have a job? - Yes, I sell tubes.

Have you moved away from home? - Yes.

Why did you choose to move away from home? - I found living with my parents difficult and wanted my independence.

Have you ever had a life-threatening injury/disease? - No, although I fell out of a swing when I was young which was quite close to a road.

Are you currently suffering from a terminal disease/Do you expect to die soon? - No!

Do you find yourself obsessing over the idea of death, specifically the idea of a void, with reference to what may happen after death? -No.

How do you avoid thinking about death? - I try to think about my child, my job, my life.

How many evenings out of an average week do you find that you are unable to sleep because of fear of death? - One.

It doesn't matter how we die, does it? - No.

Does anyone in your family have any life threatening diseases? - My daughter is a tube.

Do you have any grandchildren? - No.

What is the achievement in your life of which you are most proud? - Juggling the requirements of being a father with my own personal needs and interests.

Have you ever been the victim of a natural disaster? - Minor earthquake which I didn't notice was going on but in the morning a tree had fallen on my bike.

Have you ever wondered what it feels like to be in a coma and thought that maybe being in a coma wouldn't be so bad? - No.

Do you often think about comas? - No.

Have you often thought about the best way to

induce a coma? - No.

Have you ever wondered about the mental experiences of someone who is in a coma? - Yes.

Have you ever thought that your whole life is a dream and that you are in a coma? - No.

How do you think time is perceived whilst in a coma? - Slowly, I suppose.

Do you have any children? - Yes, one girl, tube shape, indeterminate age.

Thank you for completing the survey. You are not eligible for any future surveys and have earned no money. Your account will be deleted shortly.

There is a sign on the door in front of me, written in marker pen on cheap corrugated cardboard. It says 'Tiny Shit Head'. I have been standing outside the door for around five minutes. It is in a part of the building I have never been to before. I had to walk down a lot of very steep steps to get here.

I have Mildred in my top pocket so she can see what is going on. I feel a vibration in my pocket. It is not my mobile phone. My mobile phone was confiscated when I arrived at work this morning. I have been given a pager to replace my phone in case my boss needs to get in touch with me.

Seems like he needs to get in touch with me now.

WHY HAVEN'T YOU LOGGED IN?

The pager is small and is held together with duct tape. It is sticky because the corners of the duct tape have folded over and the glue has been smeared over the rest of the pager. The pager looks quite old. It has dust or sand stuck to it.

Parts of my body start to sweat in this order: armpits, small of back, between legs, shoulders, under eyes, forehead, main part of legs. I can feel the sweat seeping into my well-ironed shirt, my ironed trousers and my ironed underwear. I think it is time to take the plunge and walk into my future.

I press my hand against the surface of the door and it feels grainy against my skin. It would be easy to get a splinter from this door. The lacquer is peeling away revealing ground and broken wood beneath. Shattered wood beneath pummelled lacquer.

The door opens with a series of strained groans and I find I am looking at a very dark space. Taking a step inside is tricky but I manage to move my hand around the wall and find the light switch. Yellow light creeps from a bare bulb hanging on a thread cord. It slowly grows brighter until I can make out the major features of the room.

An MDF desk, chipboard walls and a concrete floor. It doesn't feel like the right environment for shirt tie shoes jacket. It doesn't feel like the right environment for anything. There is a very old computer in here, the colour of a plastic not produced any more.

Hanging from the ceiling is a transparent plastic tube. There are no windows in the room. There are no shelves and no decorations.

My boss pages me.

```
LOG IN RIGHT NOW OR I WILL
FIRE YOU.
```

I sit down in the chair in front of the computer. The chair has a cushioned, fabric seat. It is damp. It is not the seat of a salesman. I press the computer's power button. I hear a series of whirring noises and some electrical movements.

I can't move my arms. I look at my wrists. They are bound to the chair with rusted metal hoops. There is no way I can move my hands or arms at all.

I can't remember what is happening to me.

I move forward and collapse on the bed. I feel like wet, folded paper. As I land on the bed, I feel Mildred press against my ribcage. I stand up and take Mildred out of my pocket and throw her against the wall. I make a noise.

A text message.

> WHAT DO YOU THINK YOU ARE
> DOING? PICK UP MILDRED AND
> LOOK AFTER HER OR YOU ARE
> FIRED.

I am dizzy. I pick up Mildred. I hold her up to my face and say sorry. I don't know if she can remember what happened. It seems as if my life stretches out in front of me like a sequence of repeating numbers. It feels like all of the blood is rushing away from my head and it is getting stuck in my heart.

There is no excuse for hurling your child around. I lie in bed with Mildred, curled up. I hear drunken people outside, shouting. I hear buses moving past. I sense pulsing lights through my eyelids. I feel the wind pressing against my thin windows. I feel observed.

I don't fall asleep for many hours.

Mont Thabor. Roche du Grand Galibier. Punta Cournour. Sirac. These are some of the majestic names for the soaring peaks of the Alpine mountains of France. It's difficult for me to think about the cool white slopes of these mountains. I have loved the French Alps for years, since I was very young. I think the snow and mountain air must be a very wonderful tonic against difficult modern life!

I very nearly took a job working on the slopes as a ski instructor when I was younger. The only thing that stopped me was the fact that I had never been skiing.

I think I am not going to be able to afford to go to the French Alps now I have been demoted. I am making so little money that almost my entire wage is going on provisions for Mildred and basic things to stop me from dying. Oatmeal and vegetables.

I had no idea lettuce could be so delicious.

I had no idea potatoes could be so delicious.

I had no idea the sprouts on potatoes could be so delicious.

Although I am not earning a great deal of money, I feel as though my new job is going pretty well. It is a demanding position which carries a large amount of responsibility and is high powered and executive.

I am at a travel agency. There is a lady in front of me who is dressed, I think, as a flight attendant. She is wearing a tight red dress and a tight red jacket. She is wearing a hat. She looks great. I sometimes think it would be good for my workplace to encourage the workers to wear uniforms. Is shirt tie shoes jacket a uniform?

The lady is wearing a name badge on her chest. The name badge says 'Sandra'.

'What sort of budget do you have?'

The lady has a small gap between her front teeth. I can hear a little whistle sometimes when she speaks.

'It's pretty small, really. Quite a small budget. I am trying to see what I can afford.'

'We are all trying to see what we can afford, Ian,' she keeps calling me Ian. She is great at building rapport. 'I think we need to do some probing first so I can match a holiday to your requirements effectively, Ian.'

She is really good.

'Well, I have been wanting to visit the French Alps for as long as I can remember, ever since I was very...'

'Ian, sorry to butt in, but I need to ask you some probing questions before you tell me anything about the holiday.'

'Oh, sure, no problem.'

'Ian, what do you look for in a holiday?'

'Quiet relaxation. I have quite a high-powered job so relaxation is very important in my holidays.'

'Okay, and what sort of weather do you like, Ian?'

'I like cold weather and I love mountains and

snow.'

I am really enjoying her sales structure. It is like a game of chess. It is thrilling. She is drawing the net around me. I love it. People love to be sold to.

'That's great, Ian, that's great. What sort of culture do you like to be immersed in when you are abroad?'

'Hmm. A rich culture with a history of fine gastronomy, renowned for passionate emotions.'

Sandra is tapping elegantly on her keyboard. She is biting her lower lip. I am glad that Mildred can't hear the thoughts throbbing around my brain. Mildred is in a bum-bag I have around my waist. She is asleep.

'I think I have the perfect holiday for you, Ian.'

'Yes?'

'I'm thinking: Alps.'

'Yes?'

'I'm thinking: snow.'

'Yes!'

'I'm thinking: Italy.'

'Ye-'

'I'm thinking: Italian Alps.'

A yo-yo of bile moves in my throat.

Ian's erection is poking me in the head. I am in some kind of pouch strapped to Ian's waist. I am planning my escape. I am planning my way out of Ian's life. I keep thinking Ian's name because the woman he is talking to is giving him an erection because she keeps saying his filthy little name.

I am trying to understand how I have been forced together with Ian. I was plucked from a crate of hundreds of other tubes and chosen as a sample to send to a client.

A man who looked like a pig picked me up and I was presented to Ian as part of a social experiment. I am not going to have my life ruined so that someone else can experiment on Ian. I am not going to have erections poking me in the head all day long. I am not going to listen to erotic ladies whisper Ian's name at him while he gets excited and fantasises about the sales structure.

If there is one thing I have learned whilst travelling throughout the world it is not to trust salespeople. Don't trust a single thing they say to you. Do not trust the movements of their face. If you look at a salesperson for long enough you can see the calculation behind every expression. You can see the effort required for them to pretend to have an emotional response. I can hear it in the woman's voice. I can imagine the little strings that travel from her brain to her face and pull her mouth up just so, and arch her eyebrows just so, and soften her eyes just so. Her facial expressions and voice patterns are like a foreign language she learned in school, as her brain was programmed to seem human.

Sitting at my table at home with a large piece of paper with a lot of numbers on it. The numbers represent my income and expenditure. The paper represents time, or me. It is my balance sheet.

A trip to Grenoble, near the French Alps, costs nearly £150 for the flight. The stay in a hotel will cost about £50 a night. That is about £450 for the whole week. Sandra said it was very good value for money and that prices for flights will go up soon, especially to Grenoble, which is a 'High Prestige Location'. If I'd had the money to commit to booking the trip, I would have done it. The combination of crisp snow and Sandra's sales technique made me ache to book.

I have been thinking very carefully about Sandra ever since I met her. I keep thinking about her red uniform and her red lips and her sales chart. I keep thinking about a thin crimson line that travels upwards on her sales chart. I think the crimson line is infinitely long and constantly moves upwards. A thin, piercing, crimson line. Sandra would be able to help me with my balance sheet.

I have bought a French Alps calendar and put it on the wall. I have circled November 11th on my

French Alps calendar. That is my target date. I want to be in the French Alps on that date. The picture for November is a beautiful shot of Monte Viso in the Cottian Alps.

The Cottian Alps are part of the French Alps in the south west of the range. They form part of the border between France and Italy. Maybe Sandra would come if I went there. We could stand on the border with one foot in France and one foot in Italy. I could stand in France and she could stand in Italy and we could kiss and make an international kissing partnership.

Maybe I should add a 'Kiss Sandra' date to the French Alps calendar. She might see it if she ever came round to the house. She could be there to make sure that the Actual is in line with the Target I have set myself.

I add a 'Kiss Sandra' date to the calendar. October 3rd. I feel weird. I cross out the date. I scrub out the writing as thoroughly as I can.

I hope that if I do try to kiss Sandra it will go okay. I am thinking about her red dress.

The red marks around my wrists begin to burn and suddenly I am staring into a buzzing black screen. I feel like I have negative snow blindness. The screen is vibrating in front of my eyes. My hair is falling in front of my face.

Numbers appear on the screen. They are large white numbers against a dark background. The first number is the number twenty. This remains on the screen for around five seconds. The number twenty is replaced by the number nineteen. This remains on the screen for around five seconds. The number nineteen is replaced by the number eighteen. This remains on the screen for around five seconds. The countdown continues until the number zero appears on the screen. It takes one hundred seconds for the numbers to countdown. This happens one hundred times.

The red stains in the room have almost totally disappeared. My boss's breath smells of baked iron.

It has been one month. Tiny Shit Heads have fewer targets than tube salespeople.

In the 'Targets' section of my paperwork is written:

Look after Mildred.

In the 'Actuals' section of my paperwork is written:

Mildred not looked after.

'Be honest, Ian. How do you think it is going with Mildred?'

I am not worried because I have carefully

prepared for this question. I have not prepared to fail because I have not failed to prepare. Okay, look into the eyes. Okay, position the hands in a convincing shape. Okay, rapport time.

'Mildred is healthy. I am happy. We give each other strength. We need each other. We love each other.'

My boss has his face in his hands. He is not making any noise at all and is totally still. I think his organs may have stopped for a second. Oh dear. I think his organs are going to start working very effectively in a second.

He is looking at me, totally disgusted.

'Ian. You are an idiot.'

My boss knows what's best for me.

'Do you even understand why I have given you this project, Ian? You are not meant to feel love and fulfilment. You are meant to feel ashamed of yourself. You are meant to hit your targets. Have you been showing Mildred to everyone you meet?'

I have not prepared for this question. I have prepared to fail.

'Yes.'

'In all the time you have worked here you have been incompetent and negligent, but this is the first time you haven't been honest, Ian. I know you haven't been showing Mildred to everyone you meet.'

'Oh.'

'I know everything you have been doing with Mildred. Have you told your family about her?'

'No.'

'I know you haven't. I am going to let you in on a secret.'

I have always wanted to be the confidant of someone whom I hold in high regard. There was a boy in school who used to tell me secrets. He used to hide his work from the teachers and pretend that he had lost it. I never broke his confidence.

'I will keep your secret, I promise.' I say, my voice lowered.

My boss winces before getting up from his desk. He looks at me. He looks away from me. He walks up to one of the walls before touching a section of it with his right hand.

There is a noise from a science fiction film and some kind of movement. A door-shaped hole opens in the wall. I can hear metal noises coming from beyond the door-shaped hole. Metal scraping against other metal.

'Aren't you going to have a look?'

I walk over to the door and look inside. There is a desk. There is a chair. There are fifteen monitors. Fourteen of the monitors are showing views covering every possible angle of the interior of my house. The other monitor is labelled 'MildredCam'.

It is dark in there.

I take Mildred out of the bum-bag and hold her up to my face. I look at the screen of MildredCam. I am on MildredCam. I am the star of MildredCam.

There is a big sign above the Ian Observation Pod. It says: Ian Observation Pod. I close my eyes, press my hand hard into my forehead and then open my eyes. I feel like five years have been taken away from my life.

'Pretty sweet rig?' He says.

'Impressive.' I say.

'Now you know how important you are to me, Ian. You remind me of myself, but more observed. A more observed, poorer version of me. How do you feel, knowing that you are so carefully observed?'

'Important.'

'You are important to me, Ian. You are my project. That's why you have to follow my instructions about Mildred. Otherwise you are going to be with her for a very long time.'

'Well, I am her father.'

My boss leaps across the room and pins me up against the wall of monitors. His angry face is illuminated by the light from inside my flat and he screams at me.

'You are not Mildred's fucking father. Mildred is a fucking tube and you have to pretend that she is a fucking baby! Do you understand? A tube isn't your fucking baby.'

I don't know what to do.

'This is what you are aiming for, Okay? Shame. Guilt. Shame. Guilt.' He is shouting these words into my face over and over again. Numbers count down from twenty in my mind as he repeats the words over and over again into my face. He repeats the words one hundred times.

'Hi, this is my baby, Mildred. She's almost one year old and she is starting to make sounds which are nearly words! I am really proud of her and I am very much the doting father.'

The girl looks at me as though I am totally crazy. I feel like I am becoming totally crazy.

'Okay. Do you mind if I give you your change in pound coins? I don't have any five pound notes.'

'I don't know, I'll have to check with Mildred! If you remember, that's my baby's name.'

I lower the lid of the pram and look carefully at Mildred.

'What do you think, Mildred? Are pound coins okay? Ha ha ha. You must think I am mad. It's just so amazing being a father.'

Mildred is a grey tube lying down on pink sheets in a pram. Pinned up on the wall of the inside of the pram is a photo of the French Alps. Mildred is not covered by any sheets. She is a hardy Chinese tube.

'It must be great.' The girl seems to be empathising.

'Thanks. You must be a little young to have children?'

'I'm fourteen.'

Even small talk like this is a fantastic way to build up my rapport skills. Time for a joke to make an immediate connection that transcends language.

'Well, you never know these days!'

'Are you saying I'm a slut?'

'Of course not, Sandra.'

'I'm not called Sandra.'

'I mean, of course not, Sandra is my wife. Ha ha ha!'

It is difficult having normal social interactions with people when I take a small grey tube with me wherever I go. The main problem is that they think I am mad.

I am walking home through the city and it is starting to rain. I am worried about slipping and pushing Mildred into the middle of the road. There are leaves on the ground and they are making me slip. The rain gets heavier. I put up the hood of the pram and start to walk faster towards home. There is a lot of water on the ground.

I imagine the water rising so fast that I have to struggle to keep moving. All of the filth of the pavement licking at my skin. The water will rise all the way up to the bottom of the pram. The water will carry on rising upwards. I will be covered in sewage and the pram will float away into the distance. I will be suffocated by layers of mud, chewing gum, leaves, earth, thick grey dust, bird mess, nails, rusted iron. I will be screaming as I drown.

Mildred is the only thing that will survive and she will repopulate the planet.

I happen to be sitting on a bench facing the travel agency. It is five thirty, the time Sandra finishes her working day. I am casually reading the newspaper on a Saturday afternoon after going shopping.

Sandra is not wearing a red flight attendant's uniform today, or maybe she has changed out of it. I am thinking about Sandra changing out of her uniform.

She is dressed normally, she is wearing casual clothes, she has a bag, she is walking away from the travel agency. She is turning into *** street.

That is on my way home.

Walking behind Sandra on my way home and her way home. There are many people on the streets, it's the busiest time of day. All of these people in so many casual outfits. I live in the centre of the city, it keeps me corporate. I think sometimes of analogies between business and the structure of a city. Hubs and clusters. Fibre optic cables. Watching the flow of people through a city over the course of a week is very nice.

That's what I did for my holiday last year.

I took one week off and sat at different parts of the city watching things happen. I watched the morning sun rise each day, kissing the tops of the tallest buildings first and lapping down to the streets.

I watched the early commuters arrive with briefcases and red eyes, dressed immaculately and striding to their places of business; the buses opening and closing their doors, releasing people into the city; men and women handing out newspapers to the commuters.

I watched the lull of traffic as the working day began, and the crush of hungry workers at lunch time.

I watched the rain fall and felt the sun shine.

I watched pigeons walking on broken legs and eating all the food they could find.

Reflecting on the day as the hard workers lurch home with fatigue in their faces is excellent. I had learnt some people's routes by the end of the week. I was immersed in the life of normal guys. It was one of the best weeks I have ever had. I think maybe if I'd had Mildred at the time she would have appreciated it.

The French Alps will have to be incredible to top a week in the working city.

Sandra is turning down a road that isn't on my way home. I turn my head slightly to watch as she moves away from me. I adjust Mildred's new papoose and carry on towards my house. I think about my route home and Sandra's route home and the meeting point on the two routes.

I think about sales charts. Our sales charts are kissing each other. Our walking home charts are holding hands. We are building rapport with each other. We are building rapport together.

I have a dangerous thought. I think maybe I need to move forward my 'Kiss Sandra' date.

There are four tall pink walls. One of the walls is covered with a photo of the French Alps. Occasionally, Ian's gormless face ruptures my field of vision. He babbles incoherently for a while and then moves me around or puts things on me.

All I can think of is escape. I imagine freedom.

I have been rolling as hard as I can into the walls. I am trying to wear down one of the walls. I think it will take a long time because I am enviably slim and weigh next to nothing. I might wear myself away before I wear away the pram. But I don't care.

I rattle around in the pram a lot more before I give in to exhaustion.

I dream about organising a pump to squirt liquid out of me so that whenever Ian makes someone look at me I can piss all over their face.

Dear *Ian,*

You have made the best decision of your life. By ordering your AquaVeg welcome pack you have not only given yourself the chance to be fantastically healthy, but you could also make a 'healthy' profit!

Everybody knows about the health benefits of eating fresh fruit and vegetables. Everybody knows about the health benefits of eating oily fish. Respected scientist Ishiguro Morimoto made a discovery which combines these two ancient healthy foods into one ultra-modern, ultra-tasty, ultra-food.

'The flavour of an anchovy, the texture of a pear, the nutrition of broccoli. That's AquaVeg.'

You will find included in this welcome pack:
- Four packets of assorted vegetable seeds enriched with Omega 25 fish oil
- Fifty Grams of Omega 25 fish oil with applicator
- Two kilograms of genetically-enhanced fertiliser
- Five sample vegetables to show your friends
- 'AquaVeg: A Guide to Aquaticised Vegetables' 500 page instructional and marketing manual

45

This is all you need to start your very own AquaVeg business.

The way in which the AquaVeg business works is so simple and natural that anyone can run one. Everybody has friends, right? Everybody wants their friends to be healthy. You want your friends to be healthy, don't you?

Your friends need the healing power of vegetables and the natural joint lubrication accorded by the fish oil, Omega 25. It is your duty to make sure your friends know all about the incredible health benefits AquaVeg can offer.

Here's what you need to do:
- Use your fertiliser and a bucket (not included in the starter pack) to plant some of the Aquaticised seeds
- Wait three months
- Find a prominent place in your flat/house to display the healthy young seedlings
- Invite twenty or thirty of your very closest friends around for an AquaVeg experience
- Prepare a healthy meal of peppers, tomatoes, potatoes and broccoli, coated in the Omega 25 fish oil
- Tell your friends about the joyous epiphany you had the first time you tasted AquaVeg products

- Mention in passing what a reassuring sense of well-being you've experienced since the Aquaticised seedlings have sprung into existence
- Take your friends' debit card details after they have ordered a large amount of AquaVeg and forward the details to the AquaVeg company
- Wait for your 3% commission fee to arrive from AquaVeg and enjoy your new healthy, wealthy lifestyle
- Wait two months
- Persuade one of your friends to become an AquaVeg representative
- Wait for the arrival of your one-off £40 commission cheque

There is nothing immoral about forcing your friends to buy AquaVeg. You have a moral duty to ensure they experience this life-changing product. You are morally deficient if you do not take your friends' money.

Your only obligation is to buy £30 worth of AquaVeg each month for your own consumption. That means your job is to stay healthy! When people ask you what you do for a living, you have to say, 'I stay healthy, professionally!' This will get them interested and then you can effortlessly sell them a huge quantity of AquaVeg.

AquaVeg creator and CEO Ishiguro Morimoto

has the following advice for all aspiring AquaVeg
representatives:

*You are a winner, in your own
mind, because of the savoury quality of
aquatic vegetation and genetically
improved nutritional content. Harness
the power of vegetables and fish.'
      Ishiguro Morimoto PhD Ma Fsh DoD
                              PaMjKs*

Good luck and have a healthy life,

From all at AquaVeg.

The door to the house is not very welcoming. It
has no features except a peep hole. No number, no
name, nothing. This neighbourhood is not very
welcoming. The people around me do not look
very welcoming. I do not feel welcome.

I feel uncomfortable in my grey suit. I try to
clear my throat but end up making the sound of a
pig. Someone nearby laughs. The sky is white and
my mood is grim. Where am I?

My clothes have been starting to feel very
large. I feel like a boy dressing up in his father's
clothes.

I lift my fist and let it strike the door three times. It hurts a little. I don't have much fat and meat between my skin and bones any more. I stand on my scales every morning and write down a new, smaller number on my weight chart.

I don't hear anyone coming. The house is small, like an orange box. The windows have the curtains drawn so no-one can see inside. This seems the general fashion for the road.

I have Mildred with me in the bum-bag. I wipe my brow with my hand.

I wait thirty seconds before knocking a second time. I try to imbue this knock with as much positive energy as possible. I am transferring my positive energy into this household. I am preparing the household for the incredible health benefits of AquaVeg.

It would be nice if my positive energy could visibly seep into the grim-looking house. I would love the green of damp summer grass and the luscious, boiled-sweet purple of blackcurrants and the warm brown of roast almonds to gush from my knocking fist.

A cold wind whistles. I can hear movement. Time to smile. Time to engage in rapport-building.

There is a noise and the door opens. It's a small child, a girl, maybe five years old, maybe younger. She is holding a soft toy. It looks like a tube.

'Hello.'

'Hello there! Is your mummy or daddy in?'

The soft toy is an elephant.

'Yes.'

'Could you get one of them for me?'

'They want to know what you want.'

I don't know whether I can explain to this little girl about aquaticised vegetables and Omega-25 fish oil. I need to explain in simple language to her.

'I'm here to talk to them about vegetables, I have some very interesting things to show them.'

The little girl looks satisfied by this answer. She turns inside and bellows at the top of her young voice, 'Mummy, this man wants to talk to you about vegetables.'

I hear something inside, it sounds like a lady shouting out the word, 'What?'

Then she says,

'Is it Steve?'

I feel more uncomfortable than I did before.

A lady arrives at the doorway and pulls her daughter back inside. The lady is wearing a dressing gown. She has curlers in her hair. I have never seen anybody with curlers in their hair in real life before. I thought they were mainly for jokes in films I don't understand.

She looks like she was expecting me to be someone else.

'Can I help you?' she says. Time to put her totally at ease.

'No, but I can definitely help you.'

It is important to sound confident during a

sale, if you say something with enough conviction everyone will believe you and you will always make a sale.

'I don't want to buy anything. I'm quite busy.' A classic buying signal.

'I empathise and totally understand one hundred percent that you are very busy. I feel your pain, and I can identify with the disastrous plight of the modern housewife,' she makes an odd face as we build excellent rapport, 'it must be so difficult to balance getting enough vitamins from vegetables at the same time as making sure that your fish oil levels are properly topped up. How do you manage it?' This is the standard one-two: empathy, then an open question.

There is something in her face, recognition, or interest.

And then she hits me with it, smiling.

'I sell AquaVeg, too.'

I am outside my comfort zone. I feel like I am staring into a thick, semi-reflective fluid. I can see my features in the woman's face, or if not my features: my facial expressions, my tics.

The house seems to extend upwards in front of me into the sky, changing greyly into a huge skyscraper. Money pours from an open window somewhere above the lady. I can't let this excellent and respectable saleswoman manoeuvre me into a position of weakness. I am thinking about the crisp French Alps.

Mont Thabor.

'Say hello to Mildred, my newborn baby. She is just a bundle of joy and has a whole life ahead of her. She is starting to talk and makes me feel like the proudest man in the world.'

The woman is looking at Mildred.

She slams the door in my grinning face.

'You're not doing it the right way, mate.'

The phone is pressed very hard against the side of my face. I never let my frustration build up to a point where I am out of control. I am always in control of my emotions and body. The side of my face feels like it is being crushed by the phone.

'I have been following your instructions, Steve.'

Steve is the man who gave me the opportunity to be an AquaVeg representative. He showed me monochrome photocopies of his bank accounts which indicate thousands of international dollars being transferred in each month because of his AquaVeg empire. I don't think my AquaVeg empire should really be called an empire. I think it is more of an AquaVeg Welcome Pack.

The AquaVeg Welcome Pack cost me £200.

That is why I am complaining to Steve. I believe I was sold it under false pretences.

'Have you been telling your friends about AquaVeg? That should be your main source of income, Ian. As your sponsor I strongly recommend that you buy another Welcome Pack; you might have misread the instructions which could have lead to serious errors on your part.'

'I can't afford another Welcome Pack, Steve. I am trying to save up for a holiday to the French Alps.'

My leg is moving up and down of its own accord. I have lost control of my leg.

Human beings are self aware. I know I am alive because I am aware of my own, private thoughts. Decision-making is harder than thinking. My body is making decisions separate to my brain.

Steve speaks to me.

'I can go on holiday whenever I like because I have a passive income of £2,000 per month. I went to the Rocky Mountains last month and skied all the way down. Do you often go skiing?'

Why isn't he listening to me?

I become very angry. This anger comes across in the way I speak.

'Steve, I feel as though you maybe aren't using active listening to listen to me. I feel as though you maybe are not actively listening. Passive listening is really not sufficient to identify a client's needs, Steve. I am sorry to take this aggressive stance, Steve, but I have invested a lot of time and energy into this excellent business opportunity. I can't afford to lose my £200 seed money.'

I can hear something that sounds like a sigh

come from Steve. There is a brief pause in our conversation. I am preparing myself to be told off.

Steve starts to tell me off.

'You have got a bad attitude, Ian. You have the worst attitude of any of the representatives I have sponsored in the history of my relationship with AquaVeg. This is an innovative product that sells itself. It sells itself, Ian. Think about how powerful that is, Ian. Think about the power of that concept. It sells itself.'

I can feel blood pounding in my head.

Steve has a cold voice. It vibrates at the frequency of success. It is the rich and sonorous voice of a successful man. It is spit smeared on stainless steel. I can't remember what my voice sounds like.

'Remember that throughout your life you will be judged on the outcome of your actions, not your intentions. Words are not worth much. Actions and decisions are the indicators of a good man. A good man will take the decision to tell his friends about the health and financial benefits of becoming a representative of AquaVeg. Make sure you follow the path you decide for yourself. Morality and ethical preference should be defined by an internal moral compass that each one of us has. It is built in to us all; AquaVeg fine-tunes your moral compass with hydrogenated fish oils and powerful vegetable extracts. You need to believe in yourself and be true to AquaVeg in order to live a life that is fulfilling and economically viable.'

I am a child and my father is whispering reassuringly into my ear.

The words are echoes of experiences from a life I don't recognise. I wonder about self-awareness. I am aware of Steve talking to me, but I am not registering the meaning of his words. The meaning seems to have fallen away and all that is left is a hollow, shapeless space.

I walk around looking for money on the road. Mildred is in my pocket. I try not to seem like I am looking for money on the road. When I spot some, I kick it in a casual, non-committal way into a dark corner.

Then I pounce on it and shove it in my wallet!

It is much easier to get my hands in my pockets now. There is less of me to squeeze past. And less money in there to get in the way. Having less money while wanting to save money means cutbacks in other parts of life.

Wooing Sandra doesn't need to cost a lot of money. I can make her a Valentine's card out of cereal packets. I could cut hearts out of cardboard and give them to her. I could ask Steve for a loan, or try Brian from sales. I could shower her with sample tubes. She could keep her make-up in the tubes I give her.

Maybe the new boy Mark isn't new anymore

and he is making a lot of money, maybe he could give me some cash to help me get to the French Alps. After I go to the French Alps, I won't need all of this money any more. I can go back to buying bacon and other things I like.

I feel like I am about to get a pager message from my boss telling me to stop dreaming and start winning. I don't get a message. He doesn't have a camera on the inside of my head, luckily for me.

I have nothing to eat again. I find some cornflour. I boil some water. The steam from the boiling makes the windows mist up. I want to break the windows open. I pour the boiled water onto the cornflour and make a thick, fibrous paste. I eat the paste. It tastes of cornflour. I hear a thick clicking sound in front of my head. There is a scratching hiss that sounds on each click. The clicks are the beats of blood as it moves through the veins in my eyes. I open my eyes and look forward at the screen. The time is 8:29am. I am early for work. I wait for one minute, looking straight ahead. The time is 8:30am and my computer turns on with a noise. There is more noise and I am fixed into place. I think one day the machine will crush my wrists.

A message appears on the screen in thick white type against black.

'Good morning, Ian, Tiny Shit Head.'

It disappears. It is replaced by more writing.

'You have no new messages. You have no voicemail. There are no notes for you. Would you like a cup of coffee?'

'Yes, please!' I shout.

I move my head to the left and put my lips around the tube. Warm coffee comes hurtling down the tube into my stomach. It is just the way I like it. It is not just any old, instant coffee. This is freshly-brewed, delicious, ground coffee. It is a mix of smooth Arabica and rich Robusta beans. It gives a strong, thick flavour, with plenty of kick. Some people think that the best coffee is only made with Arabica beans. These people do not have an excellent palate. In order to be able to understand complex flavours you need to have an excellent palate.

And don't forget the crema!

A final line of text appears on the screen. I have seen this line of text every day for the last three months, or maybe longer. I don't know. I don't know how many times I have seen it. It is like my motto. It is engraved on my brain.

'Time for another great day at work.'

The numbers appear on the screen and start counting backwards to zero. Twenty. Nineteen. All of my favourite numbers.

Hours pass. The numbers keep tumbling down. I have two short breaks, one for coffee, one for the toilet. I make sure there are no faults with the numbers, that they are all absolutely right. My pager is quiet all day and then at half past six a message appears on the screen. The last number I see today is the number seventeen. Yesterday it was the number sixteen.

The message says,

'Any problems today?'

The hoops release my hands.

'Absolutely not.'

The final message of the day appears on the screen.

'Everything's Fine.'

I grin and suck air into my mouth. The air moves around my teeth. I grin and blow air out of my mouth. The air moves around everything else.

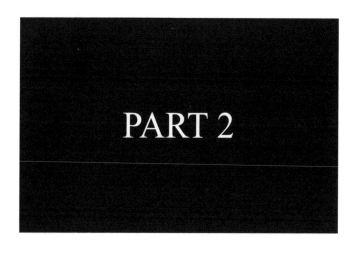

PART 2

I rest on the table each morning, watching Ian doing the same things. He emerges from his bedroom at the same time every morning. He walks through the kitchen into the living area. He is naked while he does this.

Ian's body looks fragile. He has lost a lot of weight. I can see almost every bone in his body.

I can see ribs and skull, they are moving beneath his skin. The more I can see of his human components, the less human he seems.

I feel one day he might knock himself on a door or some edge in the kitchen and shatter every bone in his body. I imagine a chain reaction of smashing, chasing from bone to bone.

I don't know what I would do with a crumpled pile of flesh and powdered bones in the flat.

Ignore it for a long time, I should think.

For breakfast, Ian has around two tablespoons of muesli. I know that half of the muesli he eats is sawdust. He buys it in bulk and uses it to increase the mass of the food he eats. I don't want to think about what it is doing to his insides. He sometimes mixes fluff from the carpet in with his food before he eats it.

He watches the morning news while he solemnly chews on his food. He makes odd noises as he eats, odd musical noises. I think this is maybe an empathetic reaction to the news stories.

He puts his head in his hands and then presses it forwards, forcing his palms over his forehead. The morning news gibbers on in the background, demented.

Ian stands and with some effort reaches up to his maximum, painful height. His stomach doesn't look like a stomach. It's usually at this point that he looks into the corner of the room. He looks straight into the corner and grins. He gives his boss the thumbs-up. The smile on his face looks unnatural. He looks sadder when he smiles.

He walks over to me and swipes me upwards before covering me with kisses. He whispers to me tenderly, his voice flaking painfully out of his throat.He puts me down and puts his suit on in the other room before coming back through, putting me in a papoose and then taking me to work. Sometimes I hear him showering in the bathroom. Sometimes I don't.

I am turning the pages of a ledger in my lap. I find the page I am looking for and write down the following.

Balancing the books:

1. Tiny Shit Head: +£590 per month
2. AquaVeg: -£30 per month
3. Online Surveys: +£1.50 per month
4. Selling old mobile phone: +£50 one-off payment
5. Selling computer game: +£12.90 one-off payment
6. Food: -£45 per month
7. Rent: -£290 per month
8. Bills: -£50 per month
9. Boss tolerance tax: -£47.25 per month
10. Equipment for Mildred: -£28 per month

Final tally = £164.15 gain each month.

French Alps trip will cost £800.

I need to save for 4.87 months in order to go to France. This does not seem like a long time at all! It seems too short.

I must have made a mistake. I rub my face with my hands. It hurts when I touch any part of my body. I feel spindly. My tendons are the spokes of a bicycle and my muscles are hard rubber. My bones are made from chalk. My eyes are a thick, white jelly. My lips are rubber bands.

There are a few things I have forgotten from my list. I can't believe I forgot such obvious items from my list!

11. Good-quality coffee: -£13 per month
12. Fish oil tablets: -£3 per month
13. Stationery: -£7 per month
14. Lottery scratch cards: -£6 per month

My new final tally is £135.15 net gain per month. This means that I will need to save for 5.9 months. Way too long. I need to find a way to make more money.

I am starting to seriously resent having to buy more AquaVeg equipment each month. I signed up for a contract. A contract is a way to trap someone into paying a lot of money for something over a long period of time. It is legally binding. There is no way to break a contract. If I were to kill myself, Mildred would have to somehow buy and consume the AquaVeg every month.

I open the drawer of the desk. There is a pad of paper in there and a pen. Time to get creative.

AquaVeg advertising slogans.

'Don't just eat vegetables! Eat vegetables covered with an aquatic paste!'

'Make yourself fitter! Be aquatic!'

'AquaVeg. Harness the savoury power of aquaticised produce!'

'Do you want your vegetables to taste more of fish? Cover them in the magnificent aquatic paste AquaVeg.'

'Not boring, very moreish, AquaVeg.'

'Feel the power. Taste the Aqua. Aquaveg.'

I am trying to get across the fact that AquaVeg is healthy, delicious and aquatic. I think I am doing well. I feel as though these are very powerful slogans. I sit back and feel the power of my slogans vibrate from the page.

I have an idea.

to: rachael.brown@rarerecruitment.co.uk
from: iantrouble@gmail.com
subject: Video Advertising Copy

Hi Rachael,

Here is my first attempt at the video advertising script for your recruitment company. Although I have a huge amount of excellent and concentrated sales experience, this is the first time I have written advertising copy for a video.

I took quite a bit of time looking around your website to get a real feel for the sort of business that you run. I was struck by how personal the website felt – I felt like you were really talking to me! Personally! I tried to reflect this in the advert script.

As I have already mentioned, this is the first time I have attempted something quite like this. If there are any minor changes that need to be made at all to the ad I will, of course, be very happy to oblige.

Please could you provide invoice details so I can get the money you owe to me?

Yours,

Ian

Advertising Copy:

Sometimes, recruitment companies bend the truth.
(graphic, 3d rotating text 'Liars')

All of them, except that is, Rare Recruitment.
(graphic, 3d rotating text 'We don't lie')

Rare Recruitment has the best levels of excellence across the board.
We provide a personal personnel (these two words need to be carefully enunciated by the actor/ress so that this endearing pun is not wasted) **service that is impossible to impersonate.**

We will find you work by exaggerating your level of experience.
(graphic, 3d rotating text 'Experience not required')

CALL NOW TO GET WORK

to: iantrouble@gmail.com
from: rachael.brown@rarerecruitment.co.uk
subject: re: Video Advertising Copy

Hi Ian,

Thanks very much for your advert script. Unfortunately, I will be unable to use the copy you have provided for us.

I feel as though you might have overlooked the fact that our company is *not* actually a recruitment agency. We provide software for the use of recruitment agencies. I also feel as though I should let you know that, this fact aside, the quality of your advert is very low and we would never be able to use it. Adverts should never have any kind of negative tone, as this is what remains in the mind of the viewer, rather than any other message. Also, your pun is totally lost over audio.

Please do not send us an invoice. We have used some copy from another freelancer.

Thanks again,

Rachael Brown

to: rachael.brown@rarerecruitment.co.uk
from: iantrouble@gmail.com
subject: re: Video Advertising Copy

Rachael,

What can I say? Great feedback. I understand and empathise 110% with your decision not to use the copy on this occasion; although verbally it is very strong, the pun could be **pun**ched up a bit (couldn't resist!). I wouldn't want us to have a **pun**ch-up.

I have another idea that might be interesting to you.

I am looking for extra freelance work at the moment. Do you need any sales people to push your recruitment software at the weekends or in the evening?

I specialise in building rapport with potential clients. I can very quickly force clients into having a natural rapport with me because of my expert understanding of the sales structure.

I am a sales professional and I want to increase my OTE by up to £25k per year. I feel I am ready for this next exciting step in my career.

Let me know.

Ian

to: iantrouble@gmail.com
from: rachael.brown@rarerecruitment.co.uk
subject: re: Video Advertising Copy

Hi Ian,

Unfortunately we do not have any sales positions in the company at the moment. We have no extra work at all.

Thanks,

Rachael.

to: rachael.brown@rarerecruitment.co.uk
from: iantrouble@gmail.com
subject: re: Video Advertising Copy

Hi Rachael,

Please keep me in mind for anything that comes up. I feel as though we have a great working relationship.

Yours,

Ian

P.S. I will consider any odd jobs around the office, cleaning for example. But don't let this put you off hiring me for a job that isn't cleaning-centric.

I am waiting for Rachael to get back to me. It makes me feel out of control. While I wait I have been concentrating on making some adjustments to the flat. I have to be ready for Mildred's maturation. I don't want her to knock her head on anything sharp or dangerous when she starts to walk.

I have added a thick layer of yellow sponge to the lowest areas of the walls in my flat. The sponge is around one inch thick and unpleasant to touch. It has caused a red, itching rash to appear on my hands.

When I was a child, I often had fantasies of living in a room that had soft walls and a trampoline floor. Children don't understand the complexities of the adult world. Mildred doesn't understand the complexities of the adult world.

There are thousands of layers of ironic and subtle nuance in adult conversation and interaction that take years to decode. Sometimes I feel as though I miss some of the ironic and subtle nuance.

Sometimes I would just like to be a child.

I have bought cheap sleeping bags. I am stapling them to the floor.

I stand by the door and look at my handiwork. I put my hands on my hips like an extremely proud builder. If someone saw me standing here they would think that I am probably a builder. They might never guess that I am a salesman!

The flat has been baby-proofed. I have made a

cardboard model of a baby to check there are no areas of the room an intrepid Mildred could get into and hurt herself in.

There are no danger zones. I think this could be the best job I have ever done.

I find it is easier to perform well if you have someone else's well-being in mind. What an odd quirk of consciousness!

It is time to check my e-mail and write a quick reminder to Rachael. I walk to the computer.

I press the lovely power button. The computer does not turn on.

Oh dear.

I have stapled the wires underneath the sleeping bags. It had seemed like a good idea at the time. I did not want Mildred to become tangled in the wires and spin downward to her death.

My protective paternal instinct impeded my objective decision-making ability.

I try to remove the wires with my hands through the sleeping bags, but I have little success. It is difficult to grip the wires through the silken, flame-retardant material of the sleeping bags.

I find my staple remover. I begin to use the staple remover on the heavy-duty staples that are attaching the sleeping bags to the floor. They are very securely attached to the floor. It feels as though someone is pulling them down who is just as strong as me, pulling them up. Maybe these staples have a section that melts as they go into the ground to give them extra adhesive ability.

I pull up the first staple.

I am puffing and heaving. I can feel my lungs pressing my ribs outwards. I sit back with my head against the sofa, exhausted. I look around at the thirty or forty staples in the floor. I am shaking with exhaustion.

I slowly get up and put on my coat. I get Mildred. I go to the internet café across the road.

There is not a single e-mail from Rachael. I write her a brief reminder to let her know I am still interested in any extra work outside of office hours.

The sky begins to cloud over.

It's raining. Rainy days must be good for travel agencies. If I ran a travel agency then all of the sales agents would be Sandra. On rainy days I would turn up the heat to be almost unbearable. Then all of the Sandras would get into their red bikinis. They would wear their red flight attendant hats and a lovely red bikini each.

Four of them would stand by the windows beckoning people inside. We would be selling a dream of tropical perfection. Sun, Sea and Sandra. Maybe that is what the travel agency is called.

Or maybe that could be a package we offer. The *Sun, Sea and Sandra* package. One of the Sandras accompanies you on your holiday, selling you useful items as and when you need them. Sun lotion, local maps, phrase books. Everyone will go mad for *Sun, Sea and Sandra.*

I wish I could somehow get money for coming up with the idea of *Sun, Sea and Sandra.*

I move my eyes quickly over the stories in the newspaper. It is nearly the end of the day and I am getting anxious.

Today, I plan to make my move with Sandra. This could very well be the defining day of my entire existence. I will look back on this day in years to come as the day my life changed forever. The defining day of my life.

I have never made a decision before.

I suppose that is why I earn a little less money than I should. I think maybe I have insufficient courage. I don't like to take risks.

I think about the things successful people think to themselves.

Grab life by the horns.

Travel balls to the wall.

Second place is first loser.

I have around twenty minutes to wait before Sandra emerges from her office. I slowly massage my temples. I feel the breeze. I smell the rain. I am ready.

I lower the paper as I spot Sandra coming out of the travel agency. I had thought about cutting eye-holes into the newspaper like in spy films.

Six months into my relationship with Sandra I could have said, 'Here's a funny story...' and then told her the funny story about the newspaper.

I didn't have any scissors, though.

I get up and start walking in the same direction as Sandra. I know her route. I am going to cut across a certain road, and then run very fast to get ahead of her. And then I am going to walk towards her. And then I am going to bump into her and build rapport with her. And then we are going to passionately embrace and realise how much we have missed each other since our first meeting.

I am running now. People are looking at me as I run past. I leave confusion in my wake. I am a guided missile. Love is my target. Sandra is my target. The French Alps are my target.

Each footstep hurts. I think my hips and pelvis might shatter.

The city seems very worrying when you are running through it. When you notice things for just one second they seem much more menacing than when you have time to look at them properly.

Two more streets to go. I feel pretty good, except for the crippling pain in my groin and legs.

One more street to go.

Stop.

I am out of breath.

Breathing is painful. I am ejecting huge quantities of air from my lungs. I suck in a huge amount to replace it. I am heaving and retching as though I am vomiting air.

I put my hands on the wall to rest. I am looking down at the pavement. It is disgusting. It is covered in chewing gum and rusting nails and shaved sections of iron and wet rust. The person in charge of this city is not very house proud. Is it good for cities to have lots of people living in them? Maybe I could organise a marketing campaign for the city based on the continual improvement of the paving flags. It could be the central campaign statement. *Come to our city and watch a slow and steady improvement to the quality and cleanliness of the paving flags.* I think the sprint has cut off some of the oxygen to my brain.

I am less out of breath now and I lean against the wall. It is time to start walking. I walk a casual walk. I have not drunk any water today, to avoid sweating.

I am sweating.

I walk for two minutes before I notice Sandra.

She is on the other side of the road. This is a disaster. I look both ways and rush across the road. I am nearly run over by a car. The driver screams at me as he goes past. He stops his car. He is still screaming. He is screaming and beeping at me. He is getting out of his car. He looks like a body builder.

I am not a body builder and I don't know martial arts.

'LOOK WHERE YOU ARE GOING.'

'I am really sorry.'

I have to build rapport quickly here. He is walking toward me. He is storming towards me.

Out of the corner of my eye I notice that his car has a lot of dents in it. It looks like it has been in the wars. He looks like he started the wars.

As he gets closer he says things like 'Are you trying to make me kill you?' and 'You want to die, do you?' and 'What's your problem?' He pushes me and I don't say anything. He pushes me again and I say sorry.

He pushes me really hard and I stumble backwards, apologising again as I fall. The back of my head hits the pavement and then I am not aware of being there anymore. I am only aware of a dream about numbers, about blood, about rusted body parts.

Green light. White light. Green light. A hospital.

I am staring straight upwards at a ceiling. There is noise around me but I don't know what sort of noise it is. I don't know whether it is organic or mechanical.

I am trying to remember the last thing that happened to me. I am trying to understand where I am. Maybe my thoughts are not quite clear at the moment. I think I am just trying to think.

A thought is a processing of information given to you by senses.

Who cares? I'm comfortable.

How do I know if I don't exist anymore?

I rest for a very long time.

I was dropped in the road as Ian was attacked.

I rolled into the gutter. Ian rolled into an ambulance.

Some water went inside me. It came out of the other end of me.

I can feel the air flowing through me.

People walk past me all day long and I sit in the gutter carrying water from one end of me to the other end of me.

Dusting machines try to scoop me up, but I roll away from their swirling brushes.

I feel a little bad for Ian but I'm glad I got away from him because he was driving me mad.

I think I was driving him mad, too, so it's for the best.

I need to make myself attractive to plumbers so they pick me up and put me into their plumbing. I can see some guttering on the roof of a nearby building and it's driving me crazy. I am trying to not be jealous - things are a lot better than they used to be.

I am staring upwards again. Things are attached to me. They are attached to my arm, mainly. Something is around my waist. I am wearing an odd piece of clothing.

It is not totally covering me up. Someone has

taken me out of my clothes.

There is a doctor removing a large dressing from my face. My injuries were not as bad as they could have been. I could have suffered brain damage or even worse.

They have caught the man who attacked me. He is being put in prison, or whatever normally happens to criminals. Before attacking me he'd had an argument with his wife, the doctor says. That is a reason but not an excuse, the doctor says.

After I fell down, the man had continued to attack me, kicking my face.

'That's probably why your head is in so much pain.'

As the doctor talks to me, I remember back to a time I accidentally tripped up a boy in primary school. I nearly had a fight with that boy. I don't know whether my encounter with the angry man could be counted as a fight. He attacked me and I did not attack back. I don't know whether I should feel ashamed about the fact that I didn't attack back.

My face hurts. The doctor is saying something.

'Sorry, what did you say?' I ask.

'The lady who brought you here said to tell you she wishes you a speedy recovery. She gave us this.'

The doctor holds out a card. It has a word written on it. That word is my name. My name is Ian. The card says: Ian.

'Who was she?'

'A young lady. She was with you on the day they brought you in. She stayed here overnight and then went the next day, on the Sunday.'

'Oh.'

'I think seeing you get attacked like that must have really upset her. She only left after we told her you were going to be fine. You know, no brain damage or anything.'

'Oh.'

'Yes, she was really sweet.'

Sweet Sandra?

I say thank you, and the doctor leaves.

I open the envelope, noticing the way my name is written on the front. Is this Sandra's handwriting? It looks like the handwriting of a girl. It is very round and neat. The ink came from a fountain pen and is a light, watery blue. The ink doesn't know this, but it was put into a cartridge so that one day a girl could write the name 'Ian' onto an envelope, so that after a man was attacked he could be made to feel better by her kind thoughts.

I am looking at the front cover of the card. There is a picture of someone kicking a football. Underneath the picture is some text. The text says, 'Goal Kick!' I don't understand the picture on the card. I don't understand why a goal kick is important when you have been beaten up.

I open the card and look inside. There is a personal message from someone inside the card.

Dear Ian,

I am sorry about the card! All of the 'Get well soon' cards were sold out of the gift shop. This was the only one left.

I hope you get well soon,

From Sandra. (I was there on the day you were attacked)

I enter some kind of odd rapture. I let the card drop down onto my chest. I can feel my little heart beating. It is beating hard. My arms are weak by my sides.

I can't understand the feelings being generated by my mind. I am propelled vertically into ecstatic awareness. I can feel every sinew, muscle, bone, blood cell, hair, tendon, tooth and organ in my body exploding with wonder in a symphony of joy.

Then I think about Mildred. Somewhere.

Mildred. Mildred. Mildred. Mildred. Mildred.
Mildred. Mildred. Mildred. Mildred. Mildred.
Mildred. Mildred. Mildred. Mildred. Mildred.
Mildred. Mildred. Mildred. Mildred. Mildred.
Mildred. Mildred. Mildred. Mildred. Mildred.
Mildred. Mildred. Mildred. Mildred. Mildred.
Mildred. Mildred. Mildred. Mildred. Mildred.
Mildred. Mildred. Mildred. Mildred. Mildred.

I shake.

I sweat.

I cry.

I call for the doctor. Nobody comes for a long time. When the doctor comes I think about how I can explain that I have lost Mildred.

I say that I thought for some reason that I was dying. The doctor says I should see a counsellor about problems associated with being the victim of a violent assault. I say, no thanks, I am probably just being silly. The doctor says suit yourself.

I want to say: Fuck you. I have lost my daughter. I am going to lose my job because I have lost my daughter. I am not the victim of a violent crime; I am the victim of myself. Fuck you, laughing doctor. I don't need a counsellor, I need a detective. I need an expert at finding tube daughters. Fuck. Fuck.

I don't say these things.

I don't say anything. I just look to the left, and imagine how angry my boss will be.

The outside of my office looks daunting.

There are square grey pillars extending upwards. There is grey glass between the pillars. The building seems long and tall and deep. The building seems very tall. It has a huge amount of daunting, grey height.

It is Monday. I have the all-clear to return to work. My face is still swollen. It still hurts. I have taken the pain-killers prescribed by the doctor. Here is an indication of the pain and swelling on my face:

I normally pull a shirt on over my head with one or two buttons undone.

Today I had to fully unbutton my shirt and pull it on like a jacket.

The reason for this is that I did not want to accidentally touch my face with anything.

I hope you can see how much pain I am in!

I had got into the habit of arriving early in the morning, before anybody else. I had got into the habit of not looking at my surroundings.

But today, I am desperate. I stand for maybe a minute, maybe two minutes. I am thinking about what to say. I am thinking about what I need to say to my boss and I am thinking about what to say to the other members of staff.

I put my hand on the door handle and try to twist, but I don't have the strength to open it.

I lean my body against the door. I am leaning maybe twenty grams against the door. My elbow catches on the handle and I tumble into work. It hurts. I stand up.

I am at the usual junction. A sign pointing left says 'Tiny Shit Heads'. A sign pointing right says 'Normal Employees'. I pause a moment and then turn to the right. I am going into the part of the building I am not allowed to go into. I feel very weak. I push the door open and I wait for a second with my eyes closed, waiting to see my work-mates sitting at their stations.

I can hear jeering. Or cheering. I can hear humans murmuring. I can hear and feel the cold stare of the salespeople. I can hear them shouting their deals and ringing bells and celebrating and I think about my old life as a salesperson.

I open my eyes.

The room is dark and empty. The seats are all empty. The monitors are all dark. The darkness of the room seems to come from the monitors. The darkness doesn't come from anywhere; it is the natural state of things.

I walk between the pods. I look at the pods. No-one has been here for a very long time. There are insects and spiders and other things living here. There are huge cobwebs everywhere. I think briefly about ecosystems. I wonder how many flies there must be to maintain such a large population of spiders. Where do they come from?

There are piles of papers between the pods. There are remains of food and newspapers and other items that belonged to the workers. I have no idea what has happened here. It is a graveyard in here, or a museum.

I stand in the middle of the once-bustling sales office. I pick up a phone and put it to my ear. It is dead. There is no dial tone. I put the phone down on the table. A beetle crawls out of the ear piece of the phone.

There is a lift on the other side of the room.

I walk towards the lift.

I press the button for the lift and I wait. I hear some noise coming from somewhere. The button is illuminated. It has three red strips on it.

The lights on the button go out and the lift doors do not open. The lift doors are not opening.

I press the button again and the red lights come on. I wait in the cold and dark for the lift doors to open. They do not open. I am sighing a very deep sigh. It carries on for a long time then stops. Even though I have stopped sighing I continue to feel like I am still sighing.

The third button-press does not open the lift doors.

The lift must be broken. There is no note about a broken lift. I look for a number to call the lift technician. I remember I don't have a mobile phone.

I need to see my boss. He is at the top of the stairs in his office. I don't know what will happen to me if I climb all the way to the top.

The stairs are a browning, yellow colour. They are yeasty, they are yellowing, they are flaking. They remind of the 1970s. I didn't exist then. They are covered in patches of dried, sticky fluids that have been dropped by people climbing them. Coffee, tea, fizzy drinks. Covered in dust and thick grime.

I start to climb.

After just two flights, I am out of breath. The second floor is where the administrative staff used to work. It is a very unglamorous floor. I always think that administrative staff are like the foot soldiers of a company. They are the most expendable but also the most important troops/staff.

My first job for the company was working in administration. I worked in an administrative capacity. I started by moving information from a series of papers into a series of small spaces that represent papers on an electronic system. The electronic system is visually represented on a glowing screen.

It was such engaging and selfless work. It was a nice job to do. It required total concentration. Your entire body was coordinated. It was 110% obsessed with accurately transferring data from the paper to the electronic storage space.

Your brain and your body became difficult to tell apart because of the influence they had on each other.

My favourite part of the job was destroying

the papers after I had transferred all of the information onto the electronic storage space.

Ian the Destroyer.

That's what I used to think as I shredded the paper. Ha ha ha. I always shredded the paper so efficiently. Those were the days!

There is no-one on the administrative floor. It looks like they left with the salespeople. I swing open the door and peer into the murky room.

I see the row of fifteen shredders. There is so much paper in this room. So much paper that has not been shredded.

I have an idea.

I put a sheet of paper into each shredder.

I turn the shredders on at the socket.

They all shred at the same time.

The feeling I have is fifteen times as potent as shredding just one piece of paper.

I have eleven flights of stairs to climb. I am climbing the stairs with purpose. I want to climb the stairs as quickly as I can.

I had worked in administration for one and a half years. I had filed many facts and shredded many papers. One day I looked up and there was my boss. He was looking at me working and he radiated glowing rays of tenderness and care.

He said, 'You have been working very hard, Ian. We have been watching you very carefully.'

I remember feeling proud. I was surprised. I didn't think that anybody had been watching me very carefully. I was happy to carry on working in administration for a long time.

'I think it is time for your sales training, Ian. I am confident in you. I think you will be able to build rapport very effectively, Ian. You might have noticed I have put my hand on your shoulder. That is because I am building rapport with you. A physical connection means that an intellectual and emotional connection will follow soon afterwards. We are so close to having rapport, Ian. You can almost taste our rapport.'

I was stunned by his incredible rapport-building ability.

I started sales training.

I was so impressed by the secrets that were given to me at sales training. I felt as though the whole of human interaction was being explained to me. It felt like I was being given forbidden knowledge. The ability to benignly manipulate others was being passed on to me.

I was now in total command of myself. In finding myself, I found how to influence others. It turned me into an emotional weapon. It showed me that empathy and sympathy and active listening are things that you must learn.

Floor five is the sales training floor and I am there now. This is where I turned into something else. It is a place of metamorphosis. Caterpillar into butterfly. Tadpole into frog. Grub into fly. Ian into Ian.

I wish I had something to eat or drink. For a second I think about running down the stairs and out of the building to a shop around the corner. I think about drinking a bottle of Coca-Cola. I think about eating some crisps and chocolate.

My fantasies are the fantasies of a child. I think the things you want as an adult are the same things you want as a child. Except when you are a child you are not meant to know about lust and things. I think that children do have these thoughts. But because they are not sexually mature the desire is translated into a desire to put dirty things in their mouths and chew on them.

I am not a psychologist.

I still sometimes think about putting dirty things in my mouth and chewing them. I think maybe Mildred will be entering this stage at some point.

As I climb, I breathe in and out and I say, under my breath, Mildred. It is like a mantra. I imagine what would happen if I released Mildred from the top of the stairs. I don't want to think about it. I think about it for a long time. I imagine what it would be like to curl up into a tube shape and bowl myself off the top of the fifteen flights. I think it would feel better than climbing up. I think again about the inside of my body. I think about my organs, thin. Thin organs trying to keep up with the pace of my climbing. My heart, thin and stretched. Kidneys pasted to my insides, flat against my flesh. My liver is one millimetre thin. My lungs are inside out. They are breathing out when they should be breathing in. Each breath is horrible. Each step is pulling me apart. I remember a poster of a model. The model in the poster was so thin, she looked like a skeleton. I think if I saw a mirror, I would look like that. My skin is so tight over my body that I am worried it will tear. I step and step and numbers are going backwards in my mind from twenty. And I keep counting them slowly backwards from twenty.

It is making me feel better. I am repeating my favourite numbers over and over again.

It makes me relax. It feels like the stairwell is slipping away.

I imagine I am in my flat. I am sitting quietly in the corner. It is a square and grey room. There is a window and there is a door but the door I think does not work very well or maybe not at all.

There is a tiny snail in the corner.

It is pretty big for a tiny snail.

There is something about this snail. I feel as though any second the snail is going to start talking to me. Maybe this second.

'Hi, Ian.'

That is the snail. It has a high-pitched voice. It is sort of shrieking. It starts saying, 'Hi, Ian.' Over and over again.

I uncurl myself and move over to the large snail. I am not casting a shadow.

The snail is saying shrilly that I am so very thin. That I am so very thin and ugly. It is saying I should say something back to it. I am part snail, I think. I put my thumb on the snail's shell and rest it there for a second. It is a hard, shining snail. It is like hard leather. I can feel the snail's heart beating through the shell. I drive my thumb downwards straight into the heart. I give the snail the thumbs-down.

Its eyes grow bigger.

The snail is dead. I am alone with the corpse of a fantasy snail and my thumb is covered with the insides of a fantasy snail.

I have five more flights of steps to climb. I have to use my hands and arms to pull myself up, as well as my feet and legs. I must look like a crawling crab or beetle. Something with long and sinuous legs. Maybe a daddy-long-legs. I am less elegant and more out of breath than a daddy-long-legs.

The very next floor is the start of the executive levels. The executive levels are home to the most exclusive, talented and ruthless salespeople and managers in the entire organisation.

People talk about there being swimming pools up here and free, gourmet meals and other trappings of success and corporate decadence. I would like to indulge in corporate decadence. I am not in a fit state to indulge in corporate decadence.

The door is open. I walk towards the open, executive door. This floor is different to the ones below. I pull myself into the room and out of the stairwell. The room is a large, open space. There is a pit in the centre of the room. It is a large, open pit. Why would the top-level captains of executive industry be rewarded with a pit?

It looks different to a swimming pool. I move slowly toward it.

I worked for a while with a salesperson called Angus. Angus was, when I first met him, the top performing salesperson at the company. He had it all. He had wit. He had charm. He had a natural, innate ability to empathise with people.

Angus was a sportsman. Angus was handsome. Angus earned a huge salary. He was the top earner on the floor. He was promoted. He was whisked away from the lower levels and given an executive account to manage.

I haven't seen Angus for eight months. I wonder what happened to him. I wonder what happens to people who aren't me.

I become worried as I edge closer to the pit. I imagine it being full of the bodies of salespeople. I imagine hundreds of skeletons with shreds of desiccated flesh still attached and one hundred billion flies and worms slipping around in the pit, happy.

It is full of tubes. There are countless types of tubes in here. Tubes of many shades of vibrant grey, thick with dust.

If I were to fall into the pit, it might be hard to tell me apart from all of the tubes. If I did fall in, I wouldn't be able to get out.

I look around for a clue as to why all of these tubes are here. I can't see any signs or markers.

The pit is surrounded by normal looking sales pods. Could it have been a type of ball pool for the workers? I start to walk away. I notice a name-plate on one of the desks: Angus Hunter.

As I leave, I look again into the pit. I imagine jumping in. I feel jealous of the tubes.

I am telling my body there is not much farther to go now. I am co-ordinating all of my small, hard, muscles to make sure I carry myself up the final flights. Two more flights of stairs and I will be there.

I round the bend to the final flight of stairs. All of the surfaces I see ahead are covered in a thick layer of black, matte rubber. I am looking up at the entrance to my boss's office and it is totally black, deep and spongy. There is a plaque on the onyx door.

The plaque says in the brightest white chalk:

Little Shit Head.

I would like to go back to China, eventually. I would like to carry fluids from somewhere to somewhere else, for a long time. I am not biodegradable which means I am immortal. Eventually, I will need to be recycled but I imagine someone will carelessly throw me into the wrong bin or something. And I'll get put into the normal rubbish that goes to landfill. And by this time all of the landfill rubbish in England will be shipped off to China because of the UK being too small for all the rubbish and all the people. I will be transferred over on a huge tanker crammed with crap: tubes and wires and springs and panels of iron and smashed-up glass and I will just lie there, among it all. Then we'll arrive at my homeland and some resourceful rural worker will notice I am still pretty hardy, and he'll grab me and shove me into the plumbing. And I will carry on until this planet is dead and cold and every human being is gone. And then the sun will swallow everything up and my final act will be to carry the fire from somewhere to somewhere else. That is the life of a tube.

I knock on the door many times. The knocks are very quiet because of the rubber coating on the door. They are not so much knocks as dull thumps. Thump thump thump. I am going to walk in if there is no response after two more thumps. Thump thump. I stretch my face with a beaming grin. This is the face of a winner.

I put my hand on the door handle. The door clicks and I push.

The room is covered in the same black rubber as the entrance hall. There are twenty or thirty wall monitors slotted into the black rubber. The room is in the shape of a vertical tube. It is a cylinder.

The monitors go all the way around. The white and grey light from the monitors is giving the room an odd feeling.

My boss is suspended from the ceiling. He is in a black leather harness or a truss; I'm not sure what to call it. It looks like it hurts. His fat body is tightly strapped in. It makes him look like a piece of meat in a roasting net. He is dangling and slowly spinning. There are pieces of metal reinforcing the leather.

The expression on his face is one of total concentration. He is 110% committed to watching these monitors. I notice a sign at his eye level. It says 'Ian Observation Pod MkII'. I check the monitors. They are all views of my flat. Except for the one called MildredCam. MildredCam is not a view of my flat. It is a view of the road and of Primark. I recognise the road. I think that I know pretty much exactly where Mildred is lying.

I hear a whirring noise and my boss turns to face me. His mouth is full of tubes. There are three tubes coming out of/going into his mouth. They lead to darkened areas of the room. He says nothing because his mouth is full of tubes. He is staring straight at me.

I am grinning at him. His expression is maybe the most intense I have ever seen. I imagine him kicking my head over rugby posts. I imagine him fighting cancer and stopping it in its tracks. His eyes are straining, concentrating hard.

I think I know what is wrong.

'Hello. I know I am not meant to be up here. I know that I am meant to be working downstairs. I am really sorry.'

He looks straight at me. His expression remains the same.

'I just wanted to check where Mildred was. You probably know that I was attacked and was in hospital.'

No change.

'I'll be back at work tomorrow, anyway. I have a doctor's note until then. Sorry about being beaten up. I think I have been a lot better with Mildred, recently. I am going to get her now. Thanks for your time and really sorry to bother you.'

I think about maybe coming back to work after I find Mildred and doing half a day. Maybe I should do that.

My boss would definitely do that. He has only achieved so much because of self-sacrifice. I give very serious consideration to coming back. I won't tell him now, though, I will just show up for work this afternoon.

I am lucky to work for such a tolerant and progressive company.

My company has the desires and needs of its staff at heart.

Striving for self-betterment is the philosophy of my company and everyone who works for it.

Every afternoon of work that I do is one afternoon closer to getting to those Alps and that holiday of my dreams.

Stop drying me, Ian.

I am wrapped up in a towel. Each fibre touching me is a violation. Each scrub is an insult.

The towel is white and blue, from Primark. Ian bought it so he could dry me after he scooped me up from the ground.

Ian looks worse than before.

I don't understand him. I can't work him out. I don't understand why he would come and get me. I am a tube.

What I do know is that he has made me so miserable today that it is almost certainly the worst day of my life so far.

'I found you Mildred!'

'Let's go home!'

'I think you have grown!'

'I am your dad! Call me dad!'

'I am going to dry you!'

'You must be hungry!'

I am trying to understand emotional vocabulary and abstract responses to stimuli. My responses to stimuli rarely have any lateral or abstract reasoning behind them.

That is because I am a sensible tube, not a stupid human.

Unusual reactions are perfectly predictable.

My reaction to Ian's treatment and continued oppressive behaviour is to think of a hundred ways of escaping.

A parachuting escape, fired out of a cannon.

A rolling escape, down stairs.

A flying escape, launched by a powerfully built man.

A falling escape, out of a window, tumbling.

A melting escape, in an oven.

Those are five of the hundred ways.

I think that any escape will be okay so long as I escape as soon as possible.

Dear Sandra,

My name is Ian and I am your biggest fan! I mean it.

Can I just say first that the way you stepped in there after I had been attacked by that guy in the road was absolutely amazing?

You probably saved my life.

The doctors say that if you hadn't reacted so quickly and called them, I might have had brain damage. Thank you so much from the bottom of my heart.

Now this might seem strange to you but we have actually met once before. I was a 'punter' in your travel agency a couple of months ago enquiring about trips to the French Alps (and the Italian Alps). You might remember that I was very receptive to your sales technique (which was absolutely first rate by the way).

I am also a salesman by trade. I used to sell tubing to industrial and private companies and individuals. It's a great life, selling tubes. I am sure that selling holidays is very similar. It's quite a lonely job, I imagine!

I've had a bit of a change at work recently, a sideways move into a different department, and I have to say I do miss the thrill of closing a deal. I used to love drawing thin red lines on my sales chart all the way to the top.

I bet your sales chart is one very long red line that never stops. I bet you have the tidiest and most well-kept and beautifully organised sales chart in the whole company. I bet your Targets and Actuals are virtually identical. In fact, I bet you smash your targets every month and your boss looks at you in your assessment and is holding the paper and says, 'Sandra, once again, a perfect set of Targets and Actuals.'

Do you get your outfit especially fitted? Is it a bespoke outfit? I thought once about going into the corporate clothing business and calling the company, Nudity Solutions.

Also, what do you think about this slogan for the travel agency?

Sun, Sea and Sandra!

Feel free to tell your boss that you came up with it if you like – I owe you one since you saved my brain from damage.

I am going to pop into the travel agency at some point on Saturday to give you a gift I have bought to say thank you.

Thank you.

From Ian.

I think maybe it might be better if I take the letter with me to the travel agency on Saturday, rather than posting it. I'm really pleased with it.

It's so much easier to write your feelings down rather than speaking them out loud. My only problem now is trying to think of what sort of gift to buy for Sandra and also how to afford buying a gift for Sandra.

What do you buy for the woman who has everything?

There is a message on the beeper. Another message comes through as soon as I have looked at the first message. They read:

    WAKE UP.

    FEED MILDRED. MAKE HER GO TO
    THE TOILET. TELL HER A
    BEDTIME STORY. I AM
    WATCHING.

I look at the time on the beeper. It is half past three in the morning. Extra-curricular activities.

I make some food up for Mildred. Her favourite meal is roast beef with roast potatoes and all the trimmings. I don't have any of that. I make her a delicious meal of water and salt. It is dark in my house. I light the way with a torch because I don't want to turn on the lights and pay for the electricity.

I take a fistful of salt from the bag of salt and hold it above Mildred. I am holding her above her toilet, which is also the bag of salt. I pour the salt into Mildred and it comes neatly out of her private area and into the toilet.

Well done, Mildred.

I hold her underneath the tap and fill her up with water. She drinks and pees at the same time. What a talented kid.

I am thinking about what story to tell her.

I tell her the one about a young man who falls

in love with a princess in a pretty red outfit who works for a space company that sends people on trips to distant galaxies.

I am lying in bed and Mildred is curled up against me and I am looking lovingly at her and telling her a story and my eyes are getting very heavy. We are the same flesh and blood. There is nothing more wonderful than reading a bedtime story to a tube.

This is the fourth time I have been woken up this evening. I am thankful my boss is taking so much time to ensure the success of my parenting.

I drift into peaceful and thankful sleep. I dream about Mildred.

Today is the day!

It's Saturday. I have done everything that I need to do this Saturday. I have serviced my needs and Mildred's needs. I have been advertising AquaVeg on internet message boards.

Here is the message I write on the message boards to get people interested:

'Hi guys. What's this AquaVeg stuff everyone is talking about? Has anyone tried it? I struggle to make sure my vegetable and aquatic fish oil levels are topped up.'

Then I wait for all of the net-nerds to answer my queries. Then I direct them to my website.

Then I wait for the cash to roll in.

At work yesterday I had 'that Friday feeling'. It was Friday. It almost seemed like I was only counting the numbers down from nineteen yesterday, if you know what I mean. I wasn't. If I had there would have been serious trouble.

As 'Everything's Fine' appeared on-screen at the end of the day, I felt free and excited because I knew the next time I would be reading it would be after I had spoken to Sandra about our future together in the French Alps. I have managed to save enough for us both to go. Enough money for two tickets!

It has been a long and hard journey. I have been on a journey of emotional and financial development. I have ridden an emotional and financial roller-coaster. I am white-knuckle Ian.

I have been the perfect father.

The sun is shining today. It is washing down on me. The pavement is dry and my feet stride forward powerfully. I feel like a shark cutting through the ocean on the way to his bleeding prey.

The city in the sunshine reminds me of being a boy. Everything changed so quickly then, everything was new.

I turn down one road, I turn down another. I walk forward, I turn left. I walk forward. I have my letter and I have my Mildred.

I also have Sandra's present. It is a simple box of delicious chocolates. The chocolates are probably the most delicious chocolates that Sandra will have ever received. I have coated each of them with AquaVeg.

The only problem with telling a lady that you are in love with her is all the terrible butterflies in your stomach.

I feel like the nerves are in my brain, though, not my stomach.

I feel like I have got butterflies in my brain.

I went to the zoo once. They have a special room that is dressed up to be like the outdoors, the jungle or something.

Inside the outdoors room there are lots of butterflies. I don't know how many there are but there are a huge number. So many that wherever you look there are at least four or five butterflies in your field of vision. They fly past up and down and fast in front of you and they have such bright colours and patterns on them that you think 'Wow'. It is a reaction so direct it bypasses language and plugs itself straight into your brain and makes you think things you can't describe afterwards. A lot of the thoughts are to do with your connection to nature.

I feel like my brain is the indoor outdoor room. I feel like I am inside my brain and Sandra is there and we are being attacked by the butterflies. They are throwing themselves at us.

The butterflies keep committing suicide on us. They fly into us so fast, they die on impact.

I am being buried under millions of delicate butterfly corpses.

I open the door to the travel agency. I cannot wait for Sandra to see me and say 'Ian! It's you!' and give me a hug and talk about that time at the hospital.

Sandra isn't here. I walk into the travel agency and notice that it is very, very warm. It is unusually warm. I linger around the door and look at pamphlets and big boards that have prices and places written on them in very large numbers and letters. There are a lot of exclamation marks on the boards!

A young chap dressed in red as a flight attendant comes up to me.

'Hello!'

'Hi.'

'Can I help?'

'I am here to see Sandra.'

'I'll get her for you!'

He prances gracefully into a back room, leaving me to look at more of the brochures and leaflets and prices and names of different places I can choose to go.

Egypt seems to be the most exotic. I think about an English person on holiday, pissing on the Pyramids.

I think about the Egyptian government setting up a special kiosk to charge English people to piss on the Pyramids. I think about the Egyptian government becoming the world's most powerful government because of all the money the English pissers are giving to it.

And then I see Sandra. She is with the young chap who is pointing at me and moving his lips (talking).

She is looking at me.

OOOOOOORARARRAKRAKARKR

She is walking towards me with a succulent smile on her face. I think she is standing about three feet in front of me. Feet are an ancient part of the imperial measurement system used to measure distances. Feet are about the size of a human male foot. Feet is the pluralised form of foot. I am looking at Sandra's feet. I am looking at Sandra's face. Between Sandra's feet and Sandra's face is Sandra's body.

'Hello!'

'Hi, Sandra!'

And then I see something in her face. I see that she doesn't know who I am. Her mouth is still smiling but there is a little awkward embarrassment in her eyes. She does not mean to look awkwardly embarrassed. Her mouth and her eyes are telling me different stories.

'You are...'

'Do you remember me?'

I said that quickly because I was so upset. I try to smile like it's funny. I think I sounded very upset. I think I let her know I was very upset. I feel like all of the butterflies are gone from my mind. They have totally left, and so has Sandra. I am alone, and there is dust and silence here with me.

'Um...'

'Yeah.'

'I'm afraid...'

'Oh no...'

It might be an idea to make a joke. I don't know why she can't remember me and then I do know why.

My bloodied and bandaged face.

I think quickly about punching my face over and over again until she can recognise me.

I look at her. I don't think I want to cause her any more embarrassment.

'Oh yeah, ha ha, I came in a few months ago and we spoke about holidays to the French Alps and the Italian Alps.'

Lying is the easiest and most effective course of action. I am convincing myself. I am trying to understand why I am not telling her I am the man from the road. I am trying to understand why I can't tell her she was by my side in the hospital. I want her to remember me and see something in me that reminds her about how she felt when she wrote that card.

Instantly, Sandra seems back in her comfort zone. Back into sales mode. I am a customer again. I am a shining red dot on her sales chart. I am going to be pushed up and up on a crimson line until I reach the sun. And then the sun will turn into a larger red dot, and it will swallow me up.

'Of course! I remember! You were thinking

about the Italian Alps weren't you?'

'My name is Ian.'

'Oh yes, I know, Ian, of course. The Italian Alps, wasn't it?'

'Well, it was French or the Italian really.'

'Yes, the majestic Italian Alps.'

'We discussed France as well.'

'Mont Blanc. Monte Rosa. The Matter-horn.'

I really don't want to book a holiday to the Italian Alps. I need to let Sandra know in no uncertain terms that a holiday to the Italian Alps is totally 100% out of the question. I need to work with her and her sales structure to let her know I don't want to go to the Italian Alps.

'But I am not 110% certain it's the Italian Alps I want to go to. I think there may be other places I would like to go. And the thing is I have the money to book right now and I want to book right now. Please help me to decide.'

'I am sure that I can help you make the right decision, Ian.'

I look into Sandra's eyes. I look at her succulent smile.

One hour later I have bought two tickets to the Italian Alps. I have spent all of my money on the tickets for the Italian Alps.

Sandra does not know who I am.

I have become a victim of Sandra's sophisticated sales technique. We built amazing rapport.

Every number I see on the screen is a shit in my heart. Nineteen, eighteen, seventeen, sixteen. I see the numbers but they are translated by my brain into ITALY ITALY ITALY ITALY.

My wrists are burning inside the manacles. I have coffee inside me. I have no food inside me. The coffee only keeps me warm for a few seconds. Ten hours is longer than a few seconds.

I think, occasionally, about my boss upstairs, making sure that I am okay. I wonder how long he spends in his harness, spiralling and watching those screens. He puts in very long days, that is for sure. I get beeper messages on the hour reminding me to watch the numbers.

Sometimes he sends me a message that says:

WHY ARE YOU LOOKING AT THIS?
GET BACK TO THE NUMBERS.

I think: great trick, boss.

It is convenient for me to live inside a mental world, because I am physically uncomfortable. I use the numbers to organise my thoughts. Thirteen, twelve, eleven, ten, ten, nine, eight, seven.

Two tens?

Umm.

Panic.

I move quickly. I thrash my arms in the wrist manacles. I shake my head from side to side and I open my mouth and start shouting.

'Two tens! Two tens! Ten, ten! Two tens! Two

106

tens! Ten, ten!'

I don't recognise the voice. It is high-pitched and worrying. It is the voice of the snail from my fantasy.

I carry on until my throat hurts and parts of my body chafe against the chair. I stop when I realise I am not making any noise and I can't move because of cramp in my arms and legs.

I sweat and shiver in the cold of the white light of the numbers on the screen that carry on counting down from twenty to zero.

No-one has come. I have had no messages from my boss. The numbers are still counting down without any break. Nineteen, eighteen. Coffee?

Yes, coffee.

I don't put my mouth to the tube in time and the hot coffee spurts all over my face, then my chest, then my trousers. Even though it is not in my mouth I can still recognise the excellent quality from the smell of my face and chest and trousers.

I let the coffee soak and slowly dry on me while I feel more and more cold. I carry on watching the numbers tick down for the rest of the day.

The final number I see today is the number ten. I only see it once.

Then the message appears on the screen like every other day.

'Any problems today?'

There was a major problem and I saw the

major problem. I tried to act on the problem but nothing happened and no-one came.

'One problem.' I say, 'One repetition of the number ten at approximately 2:15pm.'

I wait for the message telling me I am fired.

I wait briefly and then a message appears.

'Please say: no.'

'No.'

The final message of the day appears on the screen.

'Everything's Fine.'

I am using the telephone to get in touch with Steve. I use a special number which means that phone calls to land lines are totally free at any time of the day or night, twenty-four hours, basically. Steve doesn't have a land line.

He says we don't need a land lines now that everyone has a mobile phone. He says he leads a life that is totally wireless. He says wires are for old people. He says that not many old people have a high residual passive income. He wishes, for their sake, that AquaVeg had been around when they were young.

He is a seriously successful guy and the top AquaVeg sponsor in the country. He has successfully built up a network of fifteen thousand

AquaVeg executive salespeople, in his region, in just four years.

He has a residual passive income of £2000 per month. That means that because of all of the hard work he has done in the past he can just sit in a bath all day and watch the money come rolling in.

He told me once that he just sits in his bath (Jacuzzi spa bath) all day long with bubble bath in it and waits for money to come pouring through the door and then he lights cigars with the money because he has so much residual passive income that he doesn't know what to do with it!

He told me that if he wanted to he could buy a golf course and live on it. He said he could live on the fairway if it was sunny or in the clubhouse if it was raining!

The best thing about Steve is that he didn't just get lucky. He put a huge amount of work into developing AquaVeg as both a brand and as a lifestyle aspiration.

The thing is, says Steve, AquaVeg isn't just healthy for you, it's healthy for your wallet! It's healthy for your residual passive income! People aspire to having the kind of life in which you don't have to do anything but watch money pouring in!

Steve says it's because we live in a consumer culture. He says it is only natural for human beings to consume everything and then want more things. That's why we need to buy more things! So we can consume them. AquaVeg is unique because you can consume it and you can also use it to make money to buy other things to consume.

It is the ultimate dream of the human beings who live in our consumer culture.

Steve says that some people ask him, occasionally,

'Why not just sell it in shops?'

He says to them, with a huge amount of confidence,

'It is too good to sell in shops. Shops would just take a percentage of the profits. They do not deserve to be able to sell this fantastic and healthy product.'

Steve is a business guru. He sets up people to sell AquaVeg but he is also a professional life coach. He specialises in improving the life of everyone who needs their life coaching.

He charges between £200 and £300 per day for his life coaching. A lot of different types of people need life coaching.

Even the most successful guys need life coaching.

Steve has a very successful and proven method for finding people who need life coaching. He looks at the figures on the London Stock Exchange or other big financial markets.

And he looks for the companies whose stocks are losing and going down and seem to have no way out. And then he rings the CEO or Director or senior managers and says,

'I will change your life. I will save your company. I will coach you back to life.'

The companies sign up extremely quickly. He is such a convincing salesperson that sometimes he can sign them up for life coaching and also get them into AquaVeg.

We have gone through a lot together, Steve and I. We have a great level of rapport and always call each other for a chat and to have a great laugh, swapping corporate stories.

Sometimes I think I am like a life coach for him. I don't charge him, though. We are friends as well as colleagues. I just help him to let off steam.

I told him this once, that I felt like I was his life coach, and he told me, in a very stern voice, that I was not his life coach and that if I did, somehow, ever become his life coach, he would kill himself.

'Steve, I have an extra ticket to go on a fantastic trip to the Italian Alps. It's for one week and includes tickets, hotel and food. We'll be staying in a little place in the Aosta Valley, with easy access to Mont Blanc, the Matter-horn and Monte Rosa. Fine food, sweet slopes, friendship. Would you like to come with me?'

'No.'

I am sitting in a brown café with Mildred across from me. I have been putting this moment off, but it's time to come clean and tell my daughter what is going on. The café looks like it might close for good any moment. The owners must have thought it would be a nice idea to own and run a café without properly looking into corporate and executive details. By this I mean location and prices and staff.

The blend of the coffee here is dreadful. It has no kick to it whatsoever. It is kick-less and bland. I need my caffeine kick! It is hard enough breaking someone's heart, but to do it when I haven't had my caffeine kick! I am sluggish when I haven't had my caffeine kick.

For a lot of people, a caffeine kick is as bad as taking heroin or some other terrible drug. They talk about it in hushed tones. They say, 'I need to get my caffeine kick,' and look at each other like they are in on a secret.

Sometimes, I say it to people of a certain type to build rapport. If someone thinks that you are in on a secret together you can build rapport very quickly and increase their tube order by up to three percent. I remember deliberately making a mistake to someone on the phone (I think I said good afternoon instead of good morning) and then I said – whoops, I haven't had my caffeine kick for the day!

We laughed and laughed and laughed and I sold.

I don't even want to look at Mildred. I am looking straight down into my inadequate coffee.

The table is sticky.

Mildred is looking happy and young. I look her in the eye and I can see she knows that Daddy is about to get serious. She is very empathetic for someone of her age. I often think that maybe she might have the gift for selling, like her Dad. Maybe I need to get her into it young.

But only if that is what she wants to do. I would never force her to do anything she doesn't want to do.

I am a serious and proud father with his daughter's best interests at heart.

Part of a child's development is to gain an understanding of other cultures and societies. For example, it is a great idea to learn about France. We are taught French in school because of the long tradition of Anglo-Franco relations.

It is not an arbitrary choice and there are no languages more appropriate for a youngster to learn.

On the other hand, it is very rare (maybe unheard of) for the first foreign language a child learns at school to be Italian. I am not saying that France is better than Italy, just that there must be a reason why French is taught to young people and Italian isn't.

I think this is why I was so keen to go to France – it would prepare Mildred effectively for that difficult time in around eleven years when she would have to start learning the tricky language of French.

I have let my relationship with Sandra affect

the intellectual development of my child. I am selfish. I just can't stifle my ruthlessly ambitious nature.

'Mildred.'

I try to keep my problems from Mildred, but sometimes it is impossible. Our lives are linked, after all. I just don't want her to grow up too fast.

'Mildred, I accidentally bought us a holiday to the Italian Alps instead of a holiday to the French Alps. Now, I know you're disappointed. I am disappointed with myself. I am really disappointed with myself. All I can do is promise you I will make the most of the holiday. We will see the peaks of the Italian mountains and we will feel the icy bite of the Italian snow. I'll make sure we have a good time on those peaks. I'll make sure we do things that make us have a good time. I could take some baguettes and other French things, so we think we are in the French Alps. Darling, I have been saving up for such a long time and I have wanted to go to the French Alps for maybe fourteen years. I can't believe I bought those tickets to the Italian Alps. I went through so much to get the money for those tickets. You went through so much. I know you have been through so very, very much. I have been feeding you salt and water for months to be able to afford it. I am so sorry. I don't know if I could go through another period of saving like that. It might be the last holiday for a long time; it might be the last treat for a long time, so we absolutely have to make the most of it. I am scared about what happens when we get back from the Italian Alps, darling. I don't know what I am going to do. My sweet girl.'

I feel a tear on my cheek. I am crying, Mildred looks very upset. I pick her up and press her against my face and I say as I breathe passionately,

'And I don't have anyone to go with. No-one is coming with me.'

And then I absolutely decide that no matter how scared and nervous and inadequate and trembling and thin I feel, I have to ask Sandra to come to the Italian Alps.

I hold Mildred out in front of my face and say to her with conviction,

'We are going to have great time together in the Italian Alps.'

Ian holds me up to his face. Ian is crying. He is telling me about his problems. He is telling me about the Italian Alps. I feel sorry for Ian. I am not going to go with him to the Italian Alps. I am an average tube, just trying to exist.

I pass a pair of older people on the road. They look happy. The lady is wearing a purple jacket and has a walking stick. The man is just an average older man with normal features. He does have a remarkable smile, though. A remarkable and very warm smile. The man is helping the old lady with her walking and the lady is looking at the man and saying 'thank you' with her facial expression.

I don't think Sandra would wear a purple coat like that. I think red is her colour. And I don't think I will ever have a remarkable smile. Maybe, if I practised very hard. I would have to practise seriously hard. I would need to take a picture of the man's face when he does the incredible smile.

Then I would tape the photo next to my mirror. Then I would practise.

I duck into an alley and take out my phone. It has a type of mirror on the back. I look into the mirror, trying to smile a remarkable smile. It is not good. It looks like I am smiling and frowning at the same time.

The travel agency is on the next street across. There are hordes of people mingling and bustling and bouncing off each other. It seems odd that so many people are in the same place at the same time. Why don't some of them just go somewhere else? Wouldn't we all be happier if there were fewer people? Maybe not. Maybe we would be lonely.

I think a lot of people still feel lonely even if there are a lot of other people around. I think this is one of the ironies of the world we live in.

I think if I was with Sandra, even if I was in a tiny place with no-one else around and I knew no-one would ever come and visit, I wouldn't be lonely for a second.

My plan is to bump into Sandra some way away from the travel agency. I don't want her to think I have been hanging around here, waiting for her. I want her to think I have a life full of dynamic sales and excellent opportunities for self-fulfilment. I want her to think of me as a family man.

I step out from the alley and into the sunlight. I am wearing my very best suit (I only have one suit). It is a thin grey suit with a lot of coffee stains. I took it to the dry cleaners and they tried their best with it. There is still a very large faded coffee stain across the trousers and the jacket. I think it gives the suit character.

I wear a black tie. I am wearing business shoes. I look like the perfect gentleman. I have splashed strong-smelling aftershave on my face and neck. I am in line with everything that adverts tell you to do to get a girl. I have left nothing to chance.

I wait, as usual, for Sandra to finish her working day. I am waiting carefully so I can see her, but she can't see me. I have Mildred tucked into my belt, out of sight. I think Sandra should not find out straight away that I have a child.

Her manager leaves first, a man with a

moustache. He wears pretty average clothes. I am sure she isn't interested in him, romantically. I am always totally clean-shaven.

There is a short wait for me now – this always happens when the manager finishes first. Maybe Sandra checks the tills or the day's figures. Maybe she is adding more and more sales to the sales chart. Maybe she has to climb a ladder to add to her sales chart.

And then Sandra is out. Whoosh!

I follow at a safe distance for two or three minutes. I don't want to scare here or make her worry about her route or anything like that. There is a moment when I think I can smell something sweet on the air. Some sweet scent, lingering as I follow.

Occasionally, through the crowd, I catch sight of Sandra's calves and I think, wow, that's Sandra!

Sun, Sea and Sandra.

Slopes, Snow and Sandra.

I turn left and walk down the street that lets me cut ahead of the walking Sandra. I start my running. Run run run. I am out of breath by the end of the running. I lean against the wall and pant and heave. I must be around thirty seconds ahead of Sandra.

While I wait, I grow nervous. I try not to think about how very tired and nervous and thin and trembling I feel, and then Sandra is there, on the same side of the pavement as me.

I walk. I am walking towards Sandra. Oh.

Sandra. Oh, I am very carefully going to bump you Sandra. Sorry Sandra.

Sorry, Sorry and Sandra.

Bump. I bump Sandra.

'Sorry!'

'Sorry!'

'Sandra?'

'Who... Ian, oh hi.'

I get a good look at her. She is crying. Her tiny and precious face is looking so very sad. She has red around her eyes.

'It's Ian, from the other day, the Italian Alps.'

'Yeah, I remember, Ian.'

'What's up, are you okay? Sorry, I mean, you don't have to...'

I am talking to Sandra and she has been crying. Is this the right time to ask her to the Italian Alps? I think it depends on what she is about to say to me.

'It's nothing, I'm fine.' She does not look fine. Maybe she is trying to pretend she is not upset so she doesn't have to spend any time with me. Then she says something else.

'You know, actually, it's not fine. It's not fine and I'm not alright.' She is heaving up her sobs now. 'I've been demoted.'

'What?'

'My boss said I have not been doing a good job recently. He said that my performance these past few months has been really bad. He said that people keep complaining that I force them into

119

buying holidays that aren't appropriate for them.'

I feel guilty.

'Do you know what he says my new job title is?'

I gulp.

'He says that from now on I am a Tiny Shit Head and I have to do all of my work from another office because I haven't been bringing money into the business. And he gave me this.'

Sandra brings out a grey plastic aeroplane around 8 inches long. It is the same type of aeroplane the travel agency has in the window. It is meant to make you think of journeys to faraway places.

'It's called Henry. I have to pretend it's my baby. I have to show it to people and pretend it's my fucking baby.'

I look at Sandra and my excitement feels like it is going to burn out of my heart and spill all over the pavement.

'Do you want to come on holiday to the Italian Alps with me? The person who was going to come, well, they can't come. It would be a shame to waste the ticket. Come with me.'

I am hoping. I am looking.

'Are you serious?'

'Yes, I am very serious. I think we have a lot in common.'

'Um.'

'The holiday is in three weeks.'

Sandra thinks about it. Her eyes close and

open and close and open again.

'I can come. I can get the time. This is so weird. I can't believe this. Are you sure? I feel like I need to do something to get away from here. I feel like I need to change something in my life. Is this some kind of odd dream? Is everything going to go wrong in a minute?'

She smiles.

'Let's go and get a coffee and talk about it. I can't just say yes to something like that.'

A latte and an Americano. Two innocent drinks for two friends who want to discuss each other and get to know each other and find out whether they want to go on a holiday to the Italian Alps together. If they do, they will probably exchange phone numbers and get to know each other in the period of time before they go on holiday.

They might even kiss each other before they go on holiday together!

'I have been a travel agent for about two years. I like it. I like giving people nice leisure activities to do. And it's good to make a sale as well.'

Sandra drinks her coffee so naturally it's almost as though she doesn't mind what she looks like when she drinks it. Sometimes, she doesn't even notice there is coffee on her top lip, before noticing and then licking it off. I can't remember the last time I have been able to casually look at someone's face this close up without being scowled at.

'My friend was doing it and she said I might like it. It's been difficult recently, though.'

Time to reply in a way designed to build excellent rapport. I want to make sure she knows I have had similar experiences to her.

'I used to work as a salesperson for a company that sells industrial tubing to clients all over the world. We bring in the tubes, sort them into different grades, and then sell them all over the place.'

'Sounds exciting.'

This is sarcasm. A classic rapport-building tool. If the other person understands that you are making a joke it makes them connect with you on an intellectual level. Like being on the same wavelength.

A wavelength is something you learn in physics at school.

I understand that Sandra is making a clever, rapport-building joke.

'It was a thrill a minute! Now I sit in front of a computer screen and watch numbers go down from twenty to zero over and over again.'

Sandra laughs. She thinks I am joking. Maybe she thinks I have a very dry sense of humour. If I have a sense of humour at all, it is almost certainly wet. It is soaking.

'I know what you mean, most jobs can feel like that sometimes. It's just figures, isn't it? Just figures on a whiteboard. You end up seeing people as numbers. I guess that's when it has gone too far.'

'Don't you like the whiteboard, though? It's nice to put up the sales information. Don't you love all the big sales going up on the chart?'

'I suppose so, but when it's not going so well, it can be kind of miserable.'

Sandra is sensitive and seems to have an elegant wisdom. I can't even try to explain how I am feeling at the moment.

'I like you, Ian. I don't know why. I liked you when you came in the first time. I liked you the second time. I thought that we hit it off really well. I remember thinking: what a nice guy.'

As Sandra says this it is like I am a helium balloon and someone who has been holding me has released me and I am hurtling upwards so fast it is impossible to keep my eyes straight. I am out of control because of helium and joy.

'And what about the time in the hospital? Crazy, eh?'

'What?'

Panic.

'What hospital? What do you mean?'

Sandra is still smiling and looking at me. Three. Two. One. Her face changes. She recognises me.

'Ian. Ian? Are you the guy who was attacked?

The guy in the hospital who I stayed with?'

I can't quite read her face. I need to say something quickly to answer her question but I don't have time to apply any kind of mental filter to the answer.

'Yes.'

And now I am looking at Sandra's face and I am starting to see a message. I think the message is that she is maybe now not going to come to the Italian Alps with me.

'Why didn't you say?'

'I was embarrassed. The other day I came in to thank you. And then you didn't know who I was. And for some reason I thought you'd be embarrassed if I told you. And then you sold me the holiday to the Italian Alps that I didn't really want, so I thought I would meet you again and tell you then. Because I was upset that I wasn't going to France.'

'What do you mean you didn't want the holiday to the Italian Alps?'

Sandra has a face that looks like a mixture of misery and fury. She has started crying again.

I want to put my arm around her.

'I just mean that I really wanted to go to the French Alps.'

She shouts at me.

'Well, why didn't you fucking tell me instead of complaining to my manager and getting me demoted? It was you, wasn't it? Why haven't you told me any of this?'

'I didn't...'

'You must be crazy if you think I am going to the Italian Alps with you. Leave me alone.'

She stands up and walks away and I know I will never talk to her again in my whole life.

And there is a huge ache inside my body and my brain. And I don't think the ache will go away. And now I am crying again and holding Mildred and wailing.

And now the barista is asking me to leave the café.

And now there is a message on my pager from my boss.

```
I WILL GO ON HOLIDAY WITH
YOU, IAN.
```

Ian has put me in the pram and has taken me for a walk. I think he has lost his mind. When I see him leering over the pram the look in his eye tells me nobody's home.

I hate my life with him.

I hate the pram.

I hate the pushing and rolling.

It is wrong to stay with someone if you are hurting or stifling yourself by staying with them.

Things just don't seem to be going right for this guy.

He doesn't know this, but today is the day I leave him for good.

I have made arrangements to get away from this life of misery. I suppose the main difference between tubes and humans is that tubes can withstand misery, indefinitely, without going mad. Human beings can only take so much disappointment and misery before their minds break apart. That's because they only have a short amount of time on the planet and because they are made of pink, mushy material. Tubes are made of Polyvinyl Chloride. Well, some tubes are – the best tubes are. I am. I am specifically formulated to resist stress-cracking. I am a polyethylene-lined, rubber-blend, chemical spray and transfer hose. Light-weight, chemical-resistant, high-specification tubing; perfect for any kind of fluid transfer.

I will blow your mind.

If you blow air through me onto your mind.

A typical joke a tube might make.

Tubes and humans often have a different sense of humour. That's because humans are not perfect. Another difference between them and tubes.

Did humans know about the tubes inside them before they designed the first tube?

I am leaving a message for Ian inside the pram for after I have gone. I am trying to leave him a message that will shake him out of his mania and maybe make him realise the life he is living is not a natural life and he shouldn't carry on with it.

I am going to leave him a simple message that he will understand – I know he will understand it because I have been his companion for this last year, or however long it has been.

If Ian had just piped me into his plumbing I would have been happy to stay with him. Ian doesn't understand about natural states.

A tube's natural state is to be part of the plumbing, or more specifically, to carry something from somewhere to somewhere else. When it is not part of the plumbing it will roll about and get in the way and be a nuisance, because it is not doing what it is meant to be doing. It is not doing what it was made to do.

The problem with humans is they don't know what they were made to do. None of them knows what their natural state is.

That is why so many of them roll about and cause a nuisance and end up not doing anything throughout their entire life.

Goodbye, Ian.

I have hated every moment I have spent with you, but it's nothing personal.

I have been going on a lot of walks whenever I have not been in work. I take the pram with me to work in the morning, in anticipation of the evening's walk.

I finish work and I go for a walk with Mildred. I put her in the pink pram and then go to the park or to an industrial part of town or just to the shops.

I wait for the holiday. I keep my chin up. I haven't spoken to anyone about Sandra. I spoke to Mildred but she can't talk back yet. Plus, she doesn't yet understand the complex affairs of the heart.

The human heart is tubes and chambers, just like an engine. I have heard people talking about that before.

On my walks with Mildred, I think a lot of things. I think of my life and I reflect on decisions I have made in the past. I sometimes have to think for a very long time before I can think of any decision I have made at all.

I think about the pressures of being a father and a role model. I think about food. I think about the turning of the seasons. This makes me think of four colours being mixed together to make grey. There are a lot of grey colours in the city. They are all different colours and they are all grey.

I think about romance. I think about Sandra. I think maybe in thirty or forty years time when Sandra and I are together that we might talk about our first ever argument in the coffee shop. Sandra will say, 'I was so silly' and I will say, 'don't blame yourself, I could have been more straightforward' and Sandra will say, 'it was lucky

I found your e-mail address and emailed you.'

I think about waiting for everything to happen. The email to come. The holiday to start. New friends to find me and come on holiday with me. To find another £800 to book a holiday to the French Alps.

I am fed up of nearly slipping over on leaves and breaking my spine apart. I leave the park and walk to the industrial part of town to look at all of the metal things. It reminds me of my work, in an odd way!

So I turn to the left and I walk for thirty minutes and I am in the industrial part of town, pushing a small pram with a tiny baby inside.

Industrial. Industrious. One word is to do with making money; the other is to do with making effort. The two are connected, but not in my case.

Sandra.

This area of town is a terrible mess of metal and rust. The metal seems to loop around the road. It is like the metal is eating the country. It is like a cage. There is a dirty river that runs through the centre of the industrial area. It is full of iron filings and copper dust, sludge and wire wool. I imagine the water is so full of crushed metal and glass that someone swimming in it would be sliced into thin strips.

I am on a bridge over the river. I stare into the water for a long time. A very long time. I imagine the bits of floating rubbish are grey aeroplanes. I imagine red-suited Sandra at the top of the river floating hundreds of the grey planes into the current and gently crying.

She is crying as she releases the planes. And now I imagine her dangling her arms into the slicing scum of the river. She takes her arms out and they are raw and bloody. I am trying to understand what the vision means.

Sandra puts her arms back in the river and grins, in pain. She collapses into the water and her flesh and blood are stripped and washed away.

The skeleton rushes past me and tumbles into a pit of tubes. Long white bones and long grey tubes.

And a huge thick piece of grey industrial tubing swings down from the scaffolding above and smashes hard into the side of the pram, knocking it flying. And I see Mildred flung from the pram, hurtling in mid-air at high speed, flying straight into the filthy water.

And I shout 'Mildred!'

'Mildred Mildred.'

I am exhausted.

I collapse on the bridge.

A torn out newspaper headline falls out of the pram. It says: Wake Up.

Flying through the air! Landing in the river!

The river leads out into the grey of the sea and the crashing waves that will carry me homeward.

Homeward bound! I will be plumbed! I can carry even the most powerful and toxic chemicals from somewhere to somewhere else! Fuck you, Ian!

HAHAHAHAHAHAHAHAHAHAHA

I feel amazing. The water fills me with a misty contentment. I am a perfect shape, I have a flawless design. I will float and slide all the way home. A victory for me and for tubes everywhere!

I am a perfect roll model!

Another typical joke a tube might make!

Don't worry if you don't think it's funny – you aren't clever enough to understand why it's so funny! And if you think you do understand it and you think it's just a pathetic play on words then you are wrong! Because you are a stupid human who knows nothing for certain and you don't even understand yourself.

I wake up.

I push the pram home with nothing inside it besides the newspaper cutting.

I open the front door and I walk into my

apartment.

I put the pram in the hallway of my apartment where I always put the pram when I bring it home, normally Mildred is inside it and I take her out but Mildred is not inside it so I don't take her out.

I walk past the pram into the bathroom.

I undo my trousers and let them drop to the floor. I let urine out of my body through my penis.

The urine splashes into the toilet.

After a period of time I finish with the letting out of urine and I tuck the penis inside my trousers and walk away from the bathroom.

I open the door to my living room.

It is a cold living room.

Because I am thin and do not have any natural insulation I always seem to be cold.

I turn on my heating and notice how quiet the apartment is.

I turn on the television and turn to a channel showing a programme about a lot of things that have happened today.

This is the news.

I stand in front of the sofa looking at the television showing the news.

I have no emotional response to the news.

I don't want to watch the news any more.

I walk to the fridge and open the door so I can look at the inside.

For dinner, I lick the inside of my fridge.

The inside of my fridge tastes disgusting.

I lie down in front of the fridge and feel tired

and cold.

I stand up and walk into the living room.

I watch more of the news until I don't want to watch any more of the news.

I watch some more of the news and now a different programme comes on about a bank.

I change the channel.

I watch adverts on the shopping channel.

I am watching an advert for a ring that has a blue gem in the middle.

The advert salesman is building rapport with me.

I change the channel in case I try to buy the blue ring.

I am hungry.

I am always hungry.

I walk up to one of the walls in my room and look at the yellow foam on the wall around the bottom.

The television is playing a programme about some kind of animal.

I look at the yellow foam.

I look at the yellow foam.

I touch the yellow foam on the wall.

I grip the yellow foam with my hands and I pull it away from the wall.

I pull the yellow foam away from the wall in large pieces.

It takes me a long time to pull it all away.

I start pulling up all of the sleeping bags.

My hands are red from the yellow foam.

I touch my wet eyes with my hand.

Now my eyes are hurting like my hand.

I have a rash on my eyes.

I walk into the bathroom where the sink and taps are.

I turn on a tap with my hand and put my face and eyes underneath it.

My eyes are covered with water and the water washes away the irritating fibres.

I turn off the tap and look at myself in the mirror.

I see a thin man with a grey face and raw, wet eyes.

I do not know who the man who is.

His eyes are blue.

Pleased to meet you, I think.

Message 1

I WANT TO COME WITH YOU TO
THE ITALIAN ALPS.

Message 2

PLEASE LET ME COME WITH YOU
TO THE ITALIAN ALPS.

Message 3

A TRIP TO THE ITALIAN ALPS
WOULD DO ME GOOD.

Message 4

I THINK WE COULD GET TO KNOW
EACH OTHER AT THE ITALIAN
ALPS.

Message 5

I AM COMING WITH YOU TO THE
ITALIAN ALPS, IAN.

Message 6

WHY AREN'T YOU GETTING BACK
TO ME, IAN? I AM YOUR BOSS.
I AM COMING ON HOLIDAY WITH
YOU TO THE MAJESTIC ITALIAN
ALPS. CALL ME STRAIGHT AWAY
TO CONFIRM THIS WITH ME OR I
WILL FIRE YOU. IF YOU DO NOT
GET BACK TO ME WITHIN TWO
DAYS I WILL FIRE YOU. I AM
BEING VERY KIND AND FRIENDLY
BY COMING WITH YOU TO THE
FUCKING ITALIAN ALPS, IAN.
GET BACK TO ME ON THE
TELEPHONE. I AM WAITING FOR
YOUR CALL. I AM WAITING FOR
YOUR IMMINENT CALL, IAN

Fourteen. Fourteen. Fourteen.
Thirteen. Twelve. Eleven. Ten.
Nine. Eight. Seven. Six. Five.
Four. Three. Two. One. Twenty.
Nineteen. Eighteen. Seventeen.
Sixenteen. Fifteen. Fourteen.
Thirteen. Twelve. Eleven. Ten.
Nine. Eight. Seven. Six. Five.
Four. Three. Two. One. Twenty.
Nineteen. Eighteen. Sixteen.
Fifteen. Fourteen. Thirteen.
Twelve. Eleven. Ten. Nine. Eight.
Seven. Six. Five. Four. Three.
Twone. One. Twenty. Nineteen.
Elevighteen. Seventeen. Sixteen.
Fifteen. Fourteen. Thirteen.
Twelve. Eleven. Ten. Nine. Eight.
Seven. Six. Five. Four. Three.
Two. One. Twenty. Nineteen.
Eighteen. Seventeen. Sixteen.
Fifteen. Fourteen. Thirteen.
Twelve. Eleven. Ten. Nine. Eight.
Seven. Six. Five. Four. Three.
Two. One. Twenty. Nineteen.
Eighteen. Seventeen. Sixteen.
Sixteen. Fifteen. Fourteen.
Thirteen. Twelve. Eleven. Ten.
Nine. Eight. Seven. Six. Five.
Four. Three. Two. One. One. Nine.
One. Nine. Everything's Fine.

'Hello, Ian.'

'Hello, my boss.'

'Thanks for getting back to me.'

'No problem.'

'I take it you received my messages regarding our holiday to the Italian Alps.'

'I did.'

'Good. It's settled. I will pick you up at 7pm and we will go together to the Italian Alps. You must be excited about going with your boss to the Italian Alps!'

'I am very excited.'

'It's a chance for you to recover some of the ground you lost because of that demotion, Ian. It's a chance for you to climb the greasy corporate pole, Ian. It's a chance to show just how good your rapport-building skills are, isn't it, Ian?'

'I can't wait to build rapport with you, Boss.'

'I can see it now. Two colleagues on the pristine slopes of the Italian Alps. The cold snow and the frosty beers!'

'I lost Mildred.'

'I know, Ian.'

'You know about it?'

'Of course I do. I have MildredCam.'

'Where is she?'

'She was in the ocean, Ian. And then, two hours ago, the signal got lost. That means she is a very, very long way away.'

'Oh.'

'Don't worry, Ian. We'll talk about it when we

are in Italy. We don't want to have fun all of the time while we are over there. We have some very, very important things to discuss. I mean, seriously important, Ian.'

'I can't wait.'

'I think that the Matter-horn is going to probably be my absolute favourite mountain, Ian. I simply can't wait to see it in real life. That odd shape!'

'Mmm.'

'Which car shall I use? They are all very expensive! Which car shall I use?'

'I don't know.'

'Ian, after this holiday, our lives are never going to be the same again.'

I hang up the phone and curl up into a ball and wait until work where I can wait for the holiday and then wait for the rest of my life.

PART 3

My face is pressed against the window, cold against the glass.

I have crushed myself into a small space in my boss's car. My body is contorted or folded somehow, like a blanket. I am only taking up around half of the seat.

A roaring buzz shines through the dark sky as a gigantic aeroplane cuts across the heavens.

I can see the underside of the plane very clearly. I think I see flames roasting from the engines, propelling it forward. I think I might be imagining the flames roasting from the backs of the engines. I can see the night sky behind the engines and I think the red and yellow against the black of the night sky is a powerful image. I think about fireworks night.

The plane is climbing into the sky. It has

hooked onto some point in the sky with a rope and it is pulling itself upwards. It is attached to a ski lift. It will climb and climb until it reaches the top of the mountain and then it will plummet downwards, carving a smooth path to its destination.

It is amazing how easy it looks for the plane to climb upwards. It is heavy; it is suspended in the sky. It looks totally natural, like the most natural thing I have ever seen. It looks more natural than the natural world. I suppose that is because it follows all of the physical rules of the natural world.

I carry on watching the plane until it flies out of my field of vision and I am left looking at the empty night.

We are on the motorway. There are three lanes of cars travelling in the same direction. The trip feels smooth. My boss has an executive and expensive vehicle. The interior of the car is matte black. There is plastic everywhere. The seats are a matte black fabric. The mats for our feet are matte black.

My boss is wearing a leather racing-driver's outfit. He looks like he is having the time of his life, driving. Every now and then he makes this noise:

Wooohhh

He then turns and looks at me and says

146

something like,

'Acceleration feels great.'

And then I have to look away from my window and say,

'Oh yeah.'

We are bonding with each other.

Blue signs rush past the car. They tell the drivers and passengers information about distances relative to the current position of the car. The distances are always approximate because not everyone is at the same distance from the sign when they read it.

A lot of people use satellite navigation systems. Everyone always wants to know incredibly accurate and up-to-date information about every aspect of their lives. I think this is because you only know you exist if someone else confirms it to you. It's especially good if an electronic intelligence confirms it to you.

My boss told me he doesn't use satellite navigation systems, for the same reason he doesn't use condoms. He says that if there is no risk of a fuck-up it's not worth doing. He is the most incredibly wise and wonderful human being that has ever lived on this planet.

The signs tell me we are getting close to the airport. I imagine I am navigating by the stars and that the aeroplanes are the stars.

My boss pushes faster and we zoom along the fast lane. I try to count the number of cars we overtake. The car we are travelling in is faster than some planes, my boss says. Some planes are very slow. The engine is so powerful the car had to be limited to 155mph. That is some serious power.

I think about the different tubes that circle around the engine. I think about all of the tubes.

I don't want my boss to see me crying.

Only one hundred miles to the airport. I wish the car hadn't been limited to 155 miles per hour.

I wish that the car could travel at three hundred thousand billion miles per hour.

I am about to wave goodbye to England. I feel anxious, strapped inside the plane. I am sitting right by the window again. The window is made of plastic. It doesn't seem very strong. Shouldn't the windows on a plane be made of steel or something?

Our take-off has been delayed. We are on the plane, waiting to take off. The sun will be up soon.

I look at my boss, sitting next to me. His eyes are closed and he looks peaceful. He looks like he is trying to sleep, maybe. We didn't talk about much in the car. We mainly just talked about the car. I hope I can keep up with my boss's banter and rapport-building. I think there is going to be some point during the holiday when we both feel comfortable with each other. I think we will look at each other and see mutual respect and admiration.

I think maybe it will be a bit awkward up until that point, but after that we will be totally on the same wavelength. That time will be called Rapport Junction.

I am looking at my boss. I look at him and hope while I am looking at him he will open his eyes and look straight at me and we will see each other looking and then we will be at Rapport Junction.

His eyes don't open. He sits there, looking perfectly overweight and moustachioed. I look at him and imagine that, instead of my boss, Mildred or Sandra was sitting next to me. I imagine Sandra holding Mildred sitting next to me.

I imagine screaming and shouting and punching and kicking my disgusting boss, who is sitting next to me like a vacuum cleaner, sucking in everything good from around him until he is so fat he turns into a black hole and destroys the universe.

I adjust my boss's blanket so he is more comfortable and warm.

An announcement tells us we are beginning to make our taxi to the runway. And then with an odd, rolling feeling, the plane begins to move.

The scenery is moving.

An air hostess is standing in front of me. She is dressed as an air hostess. I don't know what her name is but she is wearing a red air hostess's outfit. She is showing us the emergency exits on this excellent plane. One of the emergency exits is

149

right next to me. I hope there is no emergency. I wonder if air hostesses have targets. I think that they do.

My boss is sleeping right through the emergency information that the air hostesses are giving to us. What an irresponsible boss!

I adjust the air from above so it is not blowing on me. I am very cold.

The plane makes a turn and there is a rumble as the engines build power. And then we shoot forward and I am thrown back against my seat. We accelerate tremendously until I feel a thrill and the sound of the wheels against Tarmac turns into silence.

Airborne!

My face is pressed against the window. I am looking down on England. The country looks odd. It looks like a pile of metal on top of something green. Everything is getting smaller and smaller and it seems to become more and more messy and revolting. The roads and buildings are scars. The cars are parasites. I can't see any human beings from up here.

I am glad to be getting away from England. I am glad to be getting away from my work and my problems. I think that my head is spinning.

England is exactly the same as everywhere else. There are people who live there. Differences between countries seem superficial. Will my work and my problems follow me? Is it okay to want to be in a coma? Is going on holiday the same as going into a coma for a short period of time?

I think, yes, it is.

I wouldn't mind being put into a coma. I would not want any conscious thought while I am in the coma. I want it to be warm and soft. I do not want to have to build rapport in the coma or sell anything while I am in the coma. I start to think about the best way to induce a coma. I have no idea what the best way to induce a coma is.

I can see more and more green from the window. I see a spreadsheet of fields below us and the hint of a golden glow. And just as a beautiful landscape begins to emerge, we are plunged into the cloud and my view is obscured.

I wave goodbye to England. I kiss hello to the Italian Alps in Italy.

The sun is shining on me.

We are staying in a very small, chalet-type building. There are four separate double rooms. I have one of the rooms. My boss has one of the rooms. The other rooms are full of strangers.

It is snowy, everywhere.

'So, what are we going to do while we are here? What did you have in mind, Ian?'

It is starting to annoy me that my boss finishes nearly everything he says to me with my name, Ian. I know he knows what I am called.

'I wanted to go walking, mainly. See the sights.'

'Did you bring your skis or anything? We can go up the mountains and ski all the way down if you like? That's the sort of thing you do in the Italian Alps, Ian. And then in the evening time it's time for some après-ski. If you know what I mean?'

I think the reason it is starting to make me feel uncomfortable is that teachers call their children by their names a lot. It seems like he is trying to make me into a child or something. Maybe that is unfair.

'No. I don't know what you mean.'

'Après-ski means, after ski. It means getting really drunk and then finding women and having sex with them! But you can only do it if you have been skiing. Otherwise it's not après-ski. Get it?'

I mumble something to my boss about having a look around the village. I say that he can come if he likes. He says he is going to stay here and have a bath or a Jacuzzi. Or go to a nearby sauna. I say, no problem.

I wrap up warm because it is very cold and I step outside the chalet.

There are shops and lights all around. The streets have been cleared of snow and it is sort of sludgy underfoot. There is a mush of filthy ice on the edge of every road, the Italian vehicles churn it up and fling it at you if you're not careful. The snow looks disgusting, covered in muck. It is just frozen mud and grit. It is like a frozen drink you buy in the cinema that has been made to taste of soil.

I look at the shining lights of the shops. They sell snow globes and little miniature skiers. They sell all sorts of wintry types of plastic stuff. It doesn't seem charming, it just looks bad.

I feel like the gift shops should sell small, refrigerated pouches of snow, icicles and individually shrink-wrapped snowflakes.

There are bars and houses and offices and other grey buildings around the shops. There are people here who are not on holiday and live straightforward lives like I do. There are thousands of Ians who live here. I wonder what the Italian version of the name Ian would be.

Probably Iano.

I am at the outskirts of the village. There is a path leading up into the mountains. It is a snaky, thin path. There is a long stretch of snow in the distance and more and more mountains. I feel that maybe the long stretch of snow is what I have come here to see, rather than cosy little Alpine villages. I decide I am going to go for a very long walk tomorrow.

I head back into town to a camping shop. I buy very specific items for the camping trip up into the mountains. The man in the shop asks me whether I am going camping in the mountains, because it's dangerous and I shouldn't. I say no. I say that I am InterRailing and I am going camping somewhere warm, where there are absolutely no mountains.

He asks me why then have I bought very specific mountain gear.

'Okay, I am going into the mountains.'

'Be very careful, the mountains are a dangerous place.'

'Okay, I'll be very careful.'

I think to myself, I don't care if it is dangerous, I am going into the mountains to have an adventure.

I buy a lot of tinned Italian food from a supermarket. Everything is very cheap. The tinned Italian food will go very nicely with my portable gas stove. I am going to eat to like a king.

It is a fine morning in the Italian Alps. Location: Italy. I take a footstep into the snow. I am walking toward the mountains. My boss is on my right. He is wearing a fashionable ski suit. I take another footstep. I feel the snow compacting underneath my foot. Crunch. That is the sound the snow makes under my spindly weight. Cruuunch. That is the noise the snow makes underneath my boss's enormous weight.

There is a pure blue in the sky above us. The village is far in the distance behind us. The ground is white, a stretching shelf of snow, marked erratically with the thick green of the trees. There are no houses anywhere. We have been trekking for a long time already today. I am trying to block out the existence of my boss, but every now and then he says something like,

'This is so majestic, Ian. I can't get over the majesty of our surroundings.'

I secretly agree but don't reply to my boss. I am having alien feelings of resentment toward my boss. I understand that he is trying very hard to build rapport with me, but I can't quite engage with him. I think it is because I am in a coma. Maybe in a coma you have sensations but find it impossible to interpret and order that information into opinions and thoughts.

This is how I feel.

I feel confronted by nature.

I feel like an animal.

Ian is a snow fox.

Maybe I am just trying to block certain things out.

Certain things is a nice way of saying, my boss.

'Don't you think there is a certain quality to the light here, Ian? A quality you don't get in England?'

I don't look round at my boss. I carry on putting one foot in front of the other in a way that moves me forward.

Every now and then I see some other footprints, cutting across our path. Sometimes the footprints walk in the same direction that we are travelling in for quite a long time.

Each print is distinct in the snow. A wolf trying to track down a human meal could easily follow someone walking in the snow. It would be very difficult to cover my tracks. I would need a sieve full of snow on my back. The sieve would dispense snow as I move, filling in all of the footsteps. The wolf would be so angry that it couldn't find an Ian to eat!

It is nice leaving footsteps in the snow. It shows other people I have been here and that I exist. Sandra will know I exist, I think, for quite a long time. Mildred may not know I exist. I think my boss is obsessed with my existence.

I think about existence.

I have lost Mildred, my main connection to the future. I feel sad because of my lack of connection to the future.

I think, wake up.

I feel an emotion inside me. It is an emotion of abandon and impulse. I don't know the word for the emotion, but it is making me want to do something. I change my direction.

My boss says,

'Hey, Ian, have you seen something?'

He is struggling to keep up because of his body type. His body type is very different to mine.

His is 'apple-type' and mine is 'ruler-type'.

Mine is 'string-type'.

Mine is 'hair-type'.

I keep on my new trajectory and then change it again and then change it again. I am walking around in large, looping lines.

I am putting extra force into my downward footsteps to make a bigger impression in the snow.

My boss is sitting down, puffing.

'I am not going to follow you while you charge about like a nutcase.'

I think, good.

I march off toward a clump of snow-covered trees.

'I'll be waiting here when you come back to your senses, Ian.'

I have made a pattern in the snow. The pattern looks like letters. The letters spell, 'Everything's Fine'. I wrote the letters in the snow and I made the words. I leave my boss behind and head into the mountains.

I have been walking through the Alpine forest for many hours. The ground is uneven and occasionally my foot breaks through the top layer of snow and I fall a little bit through. If I broke my leg here I would be done for.

Done for is a nice way of saying I would slowly starve or freeze to death while pulling myself through the snow, screaming in agony as wolves tear pieces of flesh off my slow-moving body.

I have to make sure I don't break one of my legs. I wish I had more Omega 25 fish oil coursing through my veins. I wish I was pumped full of riboflavin. I dream of my body being encased in warming fat, the way it used to be.

I paid over £800 for my trip to the Italian Alps. I also paid thousands of calories for the trip. I suppose I traded the calories for the money. I wonder what the exchange rate between pounds sterling and calories is.

The trees in the Alpine forest are odd. The thing that is odd about them is I can't really see how far down they go. Their trunks are surrounded by snow and I don't know how deep it is. So the trees could be one thousand miles tall, for all I know. I could be on top of the deepest snow in the history of the universe. What hardy trees to have made it through all of that snow!

This area of the forest seems to have fewer trees. I think I am going to make this into my camp for the evening. It is as good as anywhere, I suppose, and there is no boss here. That's a big part of my new thing. My new thing is being a part of nature and never having to go back to work, ever again.

I unpack a special tent, one designed to be pitched on snow. The tent poles are only slightly thinner than my wrists.

I cook dinner on my stove. It is delicious. And then the work of the evening begins.

I start to dig next to one of the trees. Wearing gloves makes it tricky, but I am trying my best to get as far down as possible. I am so close to the tree that even in this cold weather I can smell the sharp sap. It smells fantastic. I can smell the snow around me. The snow and the pines and the cold are swirling over and into my body. I am taking deep breaths of air and it feels good. It feels like I am drawing the natural world inside me. There is a burning in my chest and warmth spreading through my limbs as I dig.

I dig and dig and dig.

I uncover maybe two feet of tree all the way around. I think I am close to my point of exhaustion.

I am sweating, even though I am so cold. It seems strange that my body insists on sweating, even though I know I'm in the Italian Alps. It is like my body knows something I don't.

I crawl into the tent and curl up as tight as I possibly can, snuggling cosily into the sleeping bag.

I think about the events of the day. I think about walking and letting people know about my existence. I think about the smell of the world and the cold snow around me. I think about digging in the snow and uncovering the trunk and branches of a pine. I wonder about what my life would be like if this was my real life. I think this coma is more vivid than real life. I think I want to be in a coma for the rest of my real life.

Somewhere in the distance, past the trees and the snow, I can hear someone shouting.

'Ian? Ian! Ian? Ian!'

The shouting goes on for a very long time.

I sleep through the night, undisturbed and happy.

I wake up to what sounds like a small animal, foraging next to my tent. I don't know how long I have been asleep because I have no alarm clock and my pager doesn't work on Italian mountains.

I want to investigate the animal outside. I might scare it off by getting up but that is a chance I have to take.

Sometimes, by observing phenomena, you change the nature of the phenomena you are trying to observe.

I sit up and hear the frightened sound of rapidly retreating footsteps.

I open the flaps and look around. I can't ever remember being in a more beautiful place. Layered and moulded snow, spindled tree branches, green needles scattered over the ground, a clean and calm sky, shadows from the trees above, falling below. I am somehow folded into this scene.

I emerge and take a measured lungful of air, the mysterious creature has left some tracks!

Now I have a job for the day. I am going to

pack up my gear and track down the animal, to find out what it is. I am going to follow like a woodsman: a man from television who can make fire out of sticks and logs.

I crouch down on all fours next to the tracks and put the side of my face against the snow. It feels like the right thing to do, to try to get the feel for the creature I am going to be tracking.

The tracks are very small, delicate things that made hardly any kind of impression on the snow. It looks like a craftsman has slowly traced the tracks into the snow by hand, one flake at a time. He would have had to use very tiny tools to make these tracks.

There are large gaps between the footprints, which means the creature was moving as fast as possible when it was trying to get away from me. I wish there was some way to give off messages that are easily identifiable by everything in the world. It would be great to be able to communicate exactly what I am thinking to everything and everyone that I meet, without having to worry about words.

I could have made sure the creature knew I didn't mean it any harm.

I wouldn't worry about human interaction if I had this ability. Sandra would definitely be here with me if I had been able to communicate mind to mind instead of mouth to mouth.

I would still like to mouth to mouth with Sandra.

I pack my things into the large rucksack and I am ready to track down the beast.

I walk alongside the tracks so I don't scuff them out by accident, in case I need to follow them back. After about ten minutes, I realise that my tracks and the tracks of the creature will both get me home, so I don't need to worry about scuffing the creature's tracks.

Now I am not scuffing the tracks out of respect.

I have been following the tracks for quite a long time. I am moving very slowly and methodically. I don't really want the tracks to stop. The best way to not make the tracks stop is to move slowly so they can get a long way ahead. I think about this and realise it means I will never catch up.

I look around at the forest and the snow and I don't care about never catching the creature. I feel like a creature myself.

It is interesting to look at the tracks as they change over the course of the day. They change in terms of the amount of space between the paw prints and the depth of impression. Each time there is a change I try to interpret the change. I am making a story in my mind about the kind of day this creature has had, since having a close encounter with me this morning.

This is the story so far from the perspective of the creature:

'I started out my day by looking at a strange

thing in the snow. Something moved and made a noise and I assumed it was a predator so I ran away for quite a long time. I slowed down after a while because I felt safe. I then had a break and rolled around in the snow. I was briefly accompanied by another creature which is the same type of creature as the creature I am. I changed my pace a lot due to attacks by owls and I saw a shrew.'

That is as far as I have got with my story. It is not a real story, it is a mental experiment in creativity which keeps me going as I bask in the glory of the natural world. It is important for your mind to be stimulated, as well as your senses and physicality.

The sun and its shadows show me it is late in the day. The tracks have led me deep into the heart of the Italian Alps. Far away from houses and offices and grey buildings and rust.

I am cradled by a cold, loving, wild country.

In the distance I can see more mountains and more clouds and more trees.

I look back at the tracks and start to follow them home. I feel something on my face. A flake of snow. It is snowing heavily. The trail is disappearing under the snow and I can't see anything in front of me except white.

In the middle of a blizzard. It doesn't seem so bad. I walk forward with my eyes closed. I hold my arms out in front of me so I don't bump into trees. I walk like this for as long as I feel the snow against my face.

I think for a second that if I were not in a blizzard in the Alps in Italy, the idea of being in a blizzard in the Alps in Italy would terrify me.

I imagine what I would look like from above. If someone was sitting on top of the trees, looking down at me, they would think I look ridiculous.

I realise I am laughing. I am really laughing. I am not laughing because of rapport. I am just laughing.

Ha ha ha, ha ha ha, I say. I can't stop the laughter coming out of me. Snow is going into my mouth and making me feel funny in my mouth. And that makes me laugh more and more. Ha ha ha, ha ha ha. Bumping into trees in the middle of the Alps. Covered in thick clothes, looking like some kind of Michelin Man. I feel like a pinball stuck in a faulty machine. Ding ding ding three hundred thousand points. Ha ha ha.

I would love to have someone to throw snowballs at.

I am alive.

The blizzard lasted for about an hour. I lost track of time because I didn't have a watch.

When it was over, I looked around to see how much more snow was on the ground. It looked exactly the same.

I thought for a moment about the tree I had excavated yesterday. I supposed there still would be a little excavated moat around it. Maybe. It's difficult to say, snow is quite hard to predict.

I only had around an hour or so of sunlight left before I had to pitch the tent so I looked around to see if there was a clearing nearby with enough space. I didn't see anything straight away. Then I was amazed by something.

I saw a cave cracked into the side of some rocks that made up the beginnings of a mountain. I didn't realise that caves like this actually existed. It looked like something from a film or a cartoon. A large, dark hollow with an almost perfectly round entrance.

I got out my torch and moved towards the cave. It was dry and empty inside. If I had some twigs I would have tried to make a camp fire by rubbing them into each other and putting logs on top. I thought that if I had enough food I could have lived in that cosy cave indefinitely.

My tent went up quicker than usual and within minutes I was asleep, dreaming of my adventures.

I have been woken up. I can hear something outside. It is screaming.

Ian, it is screaming. Ian Ian Ian. Why did you

leave me? I am pretty sure there is a good chance it could be my boss.

I am also pretty sure that shouting in the Italian Alps or any snow-covered mountain range is a very bad idea due to the possibility of powerful and destructive avalanches. In cartoons, avalanches always come when someone is shouting or yelping or whining loudly. I think my boss is doing all three of these things.

I am going to go and save my boss from the cold and from avalanches.

I light my torch and step outside of the cave. I shout,

'Boss!'

I hear a reply.

'Ian! Is that you, Ian?'

'Yes, where are you?'

'WHAT DO YOU MEAN? I HAVE NO FUCKING IDEA WHERE I AM!'

I don't flinch.

'Can you see my torch?'

'I don't know, flash it on and off!'

I flash the torch on and off a few times and then do it a few more times.

'Do you see that, Boss?'

'Oh god! Yes! I think that I can see that, Ian! I am coming to find you!'

My boss emerges from the darkness of the trees. I have to stifle a laugh. He is just about the funniest looking human being I think I have ever seen in my life.

He has no hat on and he is bald. His head is shining. His moustache has icicles. His cheeks are rosy red and glowing in the moonlight. He is wearing a crimson ski outfit that makes him look like a little human blimp. I think that if I pushed him over he would roll and roll and roll up lots of snow and turn into a giant snowball and eventually crush an entire village. He is a little roly-poly pushover.

'Hi, Boss, how do you do?' I say.

'I'm cold, Ian. Really cold.'

He staggers forward until finally he falls and clings on to me, hugging me and pressing his face into my body.

'What happened to you, Boss?'

He looks up at me with emotion.

'I got lost, Ian. I haven't slept. I haven't eaten. You've got all the food and the tents. I thought I was going to die, Ian. I thought that you wanted me to die.'

I pull my poor boss closer to me and put my hand on top of his head, trying to be tender.

'That's crazy, I've been searching for you, trying to find you all this time.'

I think to myself, actually, I have not thought about you at all for these past two days. It's the longest time I haven't thought about you for years. I would rather you didn't die, but your survival has definitely not been top on my list of priorities.

I have been top of the list of my priorities.

'Have you, Ian? I am so glad I found you,

mate. I am so glad. I started eating snow because I was so hungry. I tried to gnaw on some tree bark and eat snow and pine needles. I had the worst stomach pains.'

My boss's face looks a little blue.

He is a bald man who is shivering because of the cold. He is scared and cold.

He is trying to stop cancer in its tracks.

I say, quietly,

'Come on, get in the tent and I'll make you some food.'

My boss shambles miserably into the tent.

When I wake up the next morning, my boss is still asleep. I look at him inside the tent. He looks peaceful this morning. I ease myself up and leave him at base camp.

I wonder how long this cave will be our base camp.

I head out into the wilderness. I have an idea of what I am going to be doing today.

I am looking for branches of pine trees. I am looking for dry branches that don't have any snow on them and don't have many leaves. I am going to make a fire for base camp with the branches of local pine trees.

I fumble around for quite a while trying to find the right kind of branches. I know what kind of branches I am looking for. I find a tree that has a larger canopy of branches than the others and try to take as many of the larger branches as I can. I yank and twist the branches that I think I can wrest free from the pine.

Some of them are just too big and as I tug them I end up falling over backwards into the snow and making a snowy mess. When I fall over backwards, I laugh.

Before too long I have a decent collection of branches. They are not going to make any long-burning or particularly impressive fire. But they will give us some warmth for a while. There must be a way to get bigger branches, but I will worry about that later.

I head back to mission control with my arms full. I try to remember what the television log fire man was saying about starting fires with logs.

I can't really remember what he was saying. I decide I am going to do what seems sensible to me, as a human being. First, I dump all of the logs in the cave and check on my little boss. He is still happily sleeping. I can't wait for him to wake up and see I have made a fire to warm us both. It might get so warm that we will feel comfortable wearing lighter clothes. That might just be wishful thinking.

I choose one larger twig and one smaller twig. I sit cross-legged on the floor of the cave. I can't remember the last time I sat cross-legged on the floor. I think it was in an assembly at school when

I was a child. It seems pretty natural at the moment.

I wear down the end of the small stick on the ground until it is a little sharper than it was. The stick now tapers to a point. I take the larger stick.

Hang on, I think. If I do manage to make a spark and create a flame then I will need the log pile ready to go. So before I go any further I take the majority of the sticks and branches I have gathered and arrange them into an organised pile. At the centre of the pile, I put a lot of twisted up toilet paper. I am not sure whether this will work. It seems quite unprofessional.

I would love to be a professional fire maker. I don't think there is much call for professional fire makers in the corporate world.

Now I have my potential fire ready, I sit again cross-legged with my two most important sticks. I wrap toilet paper around the end of the smaller stick so that if enough heat is made it will catch alight.

I start twisting the smaller stick into the larger stick like I am trying to drill into it. I twist and twist.

This goes on for a very long time. My body is getting stronger from the Italian tinned food I have been eating. I feel like I can go on twisting for quite a long time indeed. I am twisting. There is no flame yet. I think about all sorts of things while I am twisting.

I think about all of the problems I had in

England. They don't seem important now. They seem more manageable. Then I think I didn't even want to come to the Italian Alps! I must have been mad! Who wouldn't want to come to the most beautiful place on earth? I think about the Swiss Alps. I think about the differences between my life in England and my life here, in Italy. It may as well be two different people leading these lives.

My arms are starting to ache. I wonder whether my boss is going to wake up soon. He must have been totally exhausted to sleep for such a long time. His performance has not been good! That's what I think to myself.

I think a lot about what I would do if I wasn't a Tiny Shit Head. There must be other jobs out there. Maybe I don't need a job. Maybe I can be something else. I think there are other ways to try to make people know I exist except for having a tube daughter and parading her around all over the place. Maybe there are other girls out there instead of Sandra. Maybe one of the girls will like me enough to want to make a tiny human daughter or son with her.

A tiny puff of smoke comes up from the toilet paper. I can smell burning. This makes me work harder and harder, twisting. I can see the little flame now, creeping its way away from the centre of the paper. A tiny incandescent red circle, moving outwards.

I cup the paper with my hands so the flame doesn't go out. I move over to the log pile and I carefully use the infant flame to catch light to the pieces of toilet paper in the centre.

The paper lights easily. There are flames licking around the logs in the fire. I can smell burning pine. It is a fantastic smell. The fire is starting to give out a bit of warmth now.

A smile spreads across my face and I run off into the woods to collect more wood so the fire can carry on burning for a long time.

When I return to base camp, my boss is up and sitting by the fire in his ugly, crimson jump suit. He is rubbing his hands together and breathing frosted breath out of his body. He would not be very good at avoiding attacks from wild beasts in that horrific get-up. He looks like a ready-meal on stubby legs.

The fire needs some attention so I put some more branches on. I also move some of the half-burned branches into the centre of the fire so they can get fully burned.

My boss looks warm.

'How are you feeling?' I say.

'Much better thanks, Ian. I can't believe you got a fire going. Great work. I didn't know you had it in you.'

'I know, but it sort of came naturally in the end. I was twisting for a good hour or so. I used quite a bit of our toilet paper for kindling, I'm afraid.'

My boss is quiet for a while and tries to warm his hands more in the fire. Occasionally he looks over at me with nervous eyes. I think how odd it is to see someone in unusual circumstances.

'Ian. Do you think anyone knows we are here?'

'Probably not, Boss. I think the only other person I spoke to was the man in the shop who told me not to go trekking through the mountains. But he doesn't know enough about us to worry and send search parties or whatever.'

My boss's face looks more concerned as he turns back towards the fire. The sound of the wood cracking is very loud. It is sizzling and cracking along very nicely. If it weren't for the fire, we would be in silence.

'Ian, my name is Peter. I think you can call me Peter, if you like. We've known each other for years, Ian.'

Ian and Peter.

'Okay. Well, Peter, I don't think anyone knows we are out here. I think it's quite likely we are stranded unless we can somehow find a way to get back to the chalet village.'

Another brief silence. I have a bit more time to relax in this silence and really just admire the fire. I am just so proud of it. Now, if there was a way to suspend my cooking pot over it I wouldn't even need the portable gas stove. I am so nearly self-sufficient out here. The only thing that I am really lacking is food.

'How much food do we have here, Ian?

I move over to my rucksack and look inside. There are six tins of Italian food inside the rucksack. That is enough for three days of being in this cave.

'We've got six tins of Italian food left, so that will last us for three days. I guess we could try to leave it a bit longer between meals but we will definitely need our strength to keep warm. Of course, I haven't counted the food that we can hunt and kill.'

'There's nothing here that we can hunt and kill. Why are you even thinking of hunting and killing things? How long are you planning to be up here for? We have to get back to the village, Ian.'

Peter is looking desperately at me.

'I don't think I want to.' I say.

'What?'

There is a note of pleading in his face and voice. But I don't care.

'I don't want to go back to the village.'

He looks down at the ground.

'You've gone mad.' He says.

'No, I haven't. I am happy here. I haven't been happy for years,' I am looking straight at Peter now. He looks terrified of me. 'I definitely don't want to go back to the village and I don't think I want to go back to England. I don't want to be a Tiny Shit Head anymore.'

My boss screams at me.

'This isn't about being a Tiny Shit Head or a salesperson or anything, Ian, it's about staying alive. I want to stay alive, Ian.'

I don't think Peter understands the way I am feeling. I stay silent for quite a long time, thinking about life.

I don't hear anything from my boss. He is looking down with his head in his hands. Then I notice that he is letting out a very quiet, whimpering sound.

I hear him saying that he doesn't want to die and that he wants to stay alive. He is saying that without a map we are done for.

Done for is a nice way of saying slowly starve and freeze to death while considering cannibalism.

I get up and move over to him and put my arm around him, trying to be as caring as I can. I feel bad for him. He has things in England to go back to. He has a wife and a well-paid and fulfilling job.

I comfort him. Then he starts talking to me. There is an unreal tone to his voice. It's like he is not sure what he is saying or who he is speaking to.

'Ian, we've both got lives we want to go back to. The company isn't so bad. I was really young when I started there. Twenty, I think. I was a salesman, selling the tubes. Trying to hit those targets. It was tough.'

Peter has never really spoken to me about his life before.

'Plus, not everyone is interested in tubes.'

He looks at me, crumpled.

'Then I met Jane.'

Jane is the name of Peter's wife.

'We wanted to have a baby. I worked long hours and put in extra shifts and never took my holidays. Soon the people upstairs started to notice. You don't really need much talent or ability, you just need to work really hard.'

I don't think Peter has children.

'You've got to work really hard. Make sacrifices. And so I worked and worked with blinkers on, just thinking about the tubes and then before I knew it I was this guy,'

He points to himself. He doesn't smile.

'Depressed and getting old.'

'Why are you depressed? You've got a great job. You're always telling me how much money you earn. £5.60 per second, right? You can go on holiday all of the time, wherever you want.'

I am getting angry with this man. I feel disconnected from my words.

'I look at a screen all day long watching numbers count down from twenty to zero. I get paid almost nothing. I'm the one who is depressed.'

He looks at me, wet-eyed.

'Ian. I do the same job that you do.'

'No, you don't.'

'I watch monitors all day for changes in a set of data as it follows a repeating pattern. You live the same miserable day, every day. I sit at the top of the tower and watch you all day long on all of the monitors. That's my job. I watch you shower. I watch you eat your sawdust. I watch you giving me thumbs-ups and grins all day long. I watch you walking around industrial estates. I watch you coughing. I watch you pissing. I watch you crying.'

I think about AquaVeg. I think about a chain of sponsors and representatives, stretching onwards forever. I think about Peter observing me and me observing Mildred and someone observing Peter and someone observing that person. I feel sick.

'We decided we were swapping from tubes to observation. We got rid of the salespeople. You don't need salespeople when no-one wants to buy your tubes. It feels great observing someone, doesn't it? You know what it was like with Mildred, right?'

I don't want to talk to Peter any more. The emotions I am feeling are uncontrollable. There is no strategy behind the positions my face is moving into. I can't bear it.

I shoot my boss one more look and I say one last thing. My voice is colder than the snow all around us.

'I am going to give you my phone. It has a satellite navigation system in it. Find your way back to the village and get on the plane and go back to your life of shitting on people and watching them feel miserable as you shit on them.'

I stand and turn away from Peter.

'Ian, I don't want to lose you.'

'I don't care.'

I leave my phone by the fire and I go into the tent. I zip up the tent and try to fall asleep. I can hear my boss shambling and crying and moping around outside. My sleep, eventually, is painful and full of dreams.

My first thought in the morning is that I am free.

I take my first breath as a free man. The air tastes even sweeter than it used to.

I get out of the tent and look around at the camp. It is a fine camp. Peter is nowhere to be seen. His belongings have all gone and so has my phone.

I walk over to the fire and look at the embers and ash from yesterday. There is still a tiny, red burning centre. This is so exciting. I quickly put on my coat and rush out into the trees to find more wood.

As I collect the sticks and twigs and logs, I imagine I am flying around above this scene, smiling and laughing. I feel the Alpine air on my arms and legs. My face is red and burning with cold, it feels good. I think about Mildred and wonder about the faraway land she is in now.

Maybe she didn't make it across the sea and she is now part of a coral reef. I think that whether she is part of a reef, or has been slotted into someone's plumbing somewhere, she must be happy. She must be happier than when I had to watch her every move and look after her and do all of that dreadful stuff.

Sandra is doing okay as a Tiny Shit Head, I hope. She will find a way to not do it for too long. Maybe some people like it.

I don't think anyone would like it. And if they do, then maybe they are just fooling themselves. I'm not sure. I think if people had the option to do something else then they would.

I wonder whether if I lived like this for long enough, I would get ropey arms and powerful legs, and become part of the physical universe. I do not want to be an ethereal and spindly creature any more. I want to look like I am meant to look. I want to take deep breaths and spring about and jump and kick and roll around.

I find plenty of wood but I find no food. Why don't pine trees produce a delicious, nutritionally balanced fruit? Don't they want me to live around here, indefinitely? I wonder about the little birds and the foxes. What do they eat?

After a few hours of unsuccessful searching, I head back to the camp to make the fire bigger and have some tinned food. The fire has gone out completely by now so I have to spend many calories relighting it.

I twist the sticks for hours, thinking this is good, honest work. I think about some old saying about a man chopping wood warming himself twice. I think I would rather have a pile of neatly chopped wood with a fire that never goes out. I smile at this thought and wonder whether I am wiser than the wise, old man who said it in the first place. I feel there is someone out there who I am communicating with, when I think thoughts like this. I feel like I am communicating with the amassed wisdom of humanity. It is a presence that is always around in this forest. Maybe it is not the amassed wisdom of humanity. Maybe it is the amassed wisdom of the entire Earth. Maybe I am a conscious part of the Earth. Maybe I learn things so the Earth can learn more about itself.

The fire is blazing now so it is time for supper. I realise I could have lit the fire with my gas stove. It would have been much easier than twisting sticks together. Maybe it's better to save the gas for cooking, though? I feel a little stupid, in any case.

I open the bag with the food and the stove inside it. I reach all the way inside and move my hand around. There is no food and no stove inside the bag. There is a note from Peter. It says, sorry – please forgive me. I think Peter is a miserable human being. I think that whatever forgiving thoughts I have had about him in the past were totally wrong. I wonder how we can be of the same species. I start to panic. I do not forgive Peter.

I don't know how long I have been inside this tent. I don't know how long ago Peter left me and took all of my food and my stove. I don't know how long ago my fire went out. I don't know how long ago it was that I felt cold here for the first time.

I am cold all of the time. I feel as though the cold from outside is creeping towards me. Creeping in between the gaps in the zip of the tent, creeping through the material of the tent and creeping closer and closer to me. I feel it will creep onto my skin and move closer and closer until it enters my heart and freezes my veins and arteries and the inside of my lungs and leaves me frozen here forever.

The first day after Peter left I conducted a maniacal search for food in the forest for at least twelve hours. I scratched at the bark of trees, I dug the snow until my fingers were rods of ice. I sucked at pine needles and crushed them between my teeth, I licked rocks and stones.

I didn't even find an insect I could eat.

I nearly lost the camp. If it hadn't been for the smoke from the fire I would have had to sleep under the stars, and would almost certainly have frozen to death.

For the next two days there was a blizzard so thick I was scared to step into it, even for a second. I had already started to feel weak and emaciated again.

And then I was too tired to go hunting or start fires or do anything like that. The main thing I do now is wonder how long I am going to be alive for. My main thought in the evening before I go to sleep is that I am almost certainly not going to wake up in the morning. I think that is why I am finding it so hard to fall asleep. Why do I think I am more likely to die while I am asleep?

Occasionally, I catch a glimpse of my arms or body and I think that I am blue and a skeleton again. I think maybe it has been four or five days. It could be longer. I haven't bothered to try to remember or write it down or anything. There is no point.

I am hungry. I feel like my insides are cold and thin again. I am in pain, almost constantly, from my stomach. I imagine that a creature is living inside me and is eating my organs. I imagine it crawling around in my guts and nibbling at the soft, warm intestines and kidneys and liver and bones. I imagine it sucking all of the nutrients out of me until I am a thin, grey piece of paper in the shape of a man. I am sometimes convinced I can feel its hooked feet skewering the flesh inside my body and ripping it apart. I imagine it having a bath in my hot, red blood. I imagine it using my lungs as a sauna. I feel like parts of me may stop working any time soon.

I find it hard not to think about my life in the context of being remembered. Peter will try to do everything within his power to forget about me. I think it is sad that people die and don't have people to remember them generation after generation until the end of civilisation. I am going to be one of the pile of forgotten dead. I suppose it is not amazingly important to be remembered. I think that before I was born there was no indication of me coming into existence. I am not sure whether that is relevant. I am pretty sure I am losing my powers of reasoning and understanding. I am pretty sure I am not totally with it.

It is going to be dark again soon. I am not looking forward to being alone again with my thoughts. The night is the same as the day. There is no difference. It is all silent and still. I am almost still and I am completely silent. I am forgetting about words and thoughts. I keep myself going. I don't remember walking. I don't know whether I am awake or asleep or dreaming or not dreaming or whether I am encased in an avalanche and in some tumbling, divine coma. I don't know if I am in a coma.

Nature is trying to communicate with me. It is sitting at the end of my tent and whispering things to me. It has a green head and the body of a bird. It has stars and the universe for arms and legs. Its heart is all of the humans in the world. It is whispering eternal truths about the world and all of human understanding. It keeps going on at me for hours, letting me in on unbelievable secrets about human beings, and their relationships with each other, and with the earth and the sky and fire and water.

It is speaking louder now, almost shouting. It

is telling me to wake up. I open my eyes. There is a man in my tent. He has the face of a god or some spirit. I think I am still in a coma. The man has a metal sheet. He reaches in and plucks me out and wraps me in the metal sheet and talks to me saying are you okay and hugging me to him, and over his shoulder is Peter the worm and he is looking at me, guiltily, and saying Ian we found you and crying. I am sure I am still in a coma. They are giving me things to eat and making me feel alive. They are rescuing me from my home.

I am standing outside of a door that has the words Tiny Shit Head written on it. The sign is for me. I am a Tiny Shit Head. The pager buzzes in my pocket.

> YOU ARE ONE MINUTE LATE LOG
> IN NOW OR YOU ARE FIRED.

I put my hand on the door in front of me, feeling the warped and splintered wood. I put my face against the door and breathe in as deeply as I can. I can't smell the wood, all I can smell is the chemical they have covered it with. I push the handle down and open the door.

The room is dark, as always. To my right is the yellowing, plastic switch. I flip it and the light bulb that hangs from a thread in the centre of the room zaps on and off a few times before staying lit, sweating sickly light onto the chipboard walls. There is nothing on the walls except for odd-shaped and unusually coloured stains and marks. I have wondered about cleaning them, in the past, but I don't see the point nowadays.

In the centre of the room is a small desk made of MDF that looks very un-corporate. There is an uncomfortable-looking chair sitting at the desk with odd hoops that go around the arms of the chair. A grey plastic tube hangs from the ceiling and ends at the height a man's head would be if he were sitting on the chair. There is another buzzing in my trouser pocket. This time it will be my boss going ballistic, threatening me with physical violence unless I get on with my work right away. I make my way to the chair.

I am sitting down and facing the screen of a computer the colour of a plastic they don't make any more. I press the power button of the computer and it springs to life, whirring and making oddly comforting electronic noises. Bzzz whhrrr tthhhp it says. It is on. The arm holders buzz into place. A message appears on screen in thick black type against the white.

'Good morning, Ian, Tiny Shit Head.'

It disappears.

I look down at the arm restraints. Instead of being wrapped around my arms they are wrapped around two branches of a pine tree I brought with me from the Italian Alps. The writing disappears. It is replaced by more writing.

'You have no new messages. You have no voicemail. There are no notes for you. Would you like a cup of coffee?'

'Yes, please.'

I jump up out of the seat and move my head so I can get a drink of coffee. I drink the coffee down. It is absolutely delicious, done just the way I like it.

A final line of text appears on the screen. I have seen this line of text a huge number of times.

'Enough dawdling, let's get you working!'

The numbers appear on the screen and start counting backwards to zero. Twenty. Nineteen. All of my favourite numbers.

I start whistling a happy tune and waltz out of the chipboard room. I walk out of the building and get into my car and drive home. I work on a non-fiction book while I am at home called 'The Italian Alps'. I also go for a walk and look at beautiful things. I meet a girl who attends my writing course with me. She is not called Sandra. We have coffee and talk about writing. At six thirty I go back into the office and find that there is a message on my screen.

'Any problems today?'

'Absolutely not.'

The final message of the day appears on the screen.

'Everything's Fine.'

EPILOGUE

The earth around me is cold. At one end is another tube. At the other end is another tube. Someone flushes a toilet a long way above me. I am waiting.

I count the seconds between the flush and the ecstasy. It should be twenty seconds. I can hear it coming. I can hear the thing that I am going to carry from one place to another place.

Twenty. Nineteen. Eighteen. Seventeen.

It is moving at exactly the right pace to get to me at the normal time.

Sixteen. Fifteen. Fourteen. Thirteen.

I am just throbbing with anticipation. Just so dry and ready to carry the load from somewhere to

187

somewhere else. It won't be long.

Twelve. Eleven. Ten. Nine. Eight. Seven. Six. Five. Four. Three. Two. O...

It comes at the right second. One human's worth of excrement, passing effortlessly through me and on to my neighbour. Like a dream, my existence continues. Perfect, unchanging. No beginning, no end.

Thank you to my family and my friends. Special thanks to Chris Killen, without whom this book may not exist. Thanks also to Jenn Ashworth, Tom Fletcher, Crispin Best, Gavin James Bower, Ben Myers, Adele Stripe, Lee Rourke and Nicholas Royle, for reading early drafts of *Everything's Fine*.

Thanks to Ian Carrington for writing emails, and Sarah-Clare Conlon, for her fantastic proof-reading.

Antony Edwards you are my hero.

Final thanks to my girlfriend Emma, who makes me feel brave.